Some Other Books by Joan Phipson

Birkin

The Boundary Riders

Cross Currents

The Family Conspiracy

Good Luck to the Rider

The Haunted House

Peter and Butch

Six and Silver

Threat to the Barkers

THE WAY HOME

THE
WAY HOME

Joan Phipson

A Margaret K. McElderry Book

ATHENEUM   1973   NEW YORK

THE WAY HOME

[1]

Floating up to consciousness through dark mists, the girl, Prue, did not recognize the strange landscape about her. She did not feel lost, for she knew there was nothing familiar to be found. All she did know for certain was that here—wherever it was—she was the only living thing. A long, dusty slope behind her was made up of enormous gray and black rocks and the slope below of stones of diminishing size. There were other objects besides the big rocks behind her, but she was too tired, too confused, to think what they might be. There were also strange objects among the stones on the slope in front of her, but these became smaller, like the stones, the farther down the slope they went. She somehow knew they were tremendously significant, and at any moment she would remember of what. Just now all she knew was that in a place of grayness and silence where she alone was alive, there was a huge and unbelievable desolation.

Then she found herself moving—sliding soundlessly down the hill, and for a moment everything went black. When she opened her eyes, it was to see that she was in much the same position as she had been before. There were the great rocks, the undefined objects, on the upward slope behind; there, on the downward slope in front were the smaller stones and the tree roots—statues—whatever they were, becoming tinier and tinier as they disappeared down the slope. But everything was still empty, dusty, and gray. And still she was the only living thing, and the silence lay like a blanket. She looked behind her at the great rocks and the towers, cliffs, or perhaps soaring buildings. She still could not make out what they were. But now she could see that these were the tiny stones and the vague little objects of her first position. She had shrunk and moved on, and these had taken up their position in the new landscape as the vast monoliths of this place. Those of the last place had completely disappeared. She had only just made the discovery when she moved on again, floating in blackness until a third landscape grew visible around her. This time she looked carefully at the rocks and stones, and she found that the same thing had happened again. The tiny pebbles and tree roots (if that is what they were) of her last country had grown huge behind her, heaving up ponderously against the cloudy skyline. Once more the stones on the downward slope ahead dwindled as they became more distant. Once more the desolation crept through to her bones. But now, having made what seemed a tremendous discovery, she was filled with satisfaction, and she waited with something like eagerness for her next transformation. These small stones at her feet would be the giants at her back, and she had found the answer to everything. In the new, blinding light, even her solitude ceased to matter. At last she knew; at last she understood.

4

The light grew brighter around her, blotting out the grayness of the moonlike landscape. Something moved, filled the new expanse of light, and far above and distant a voice said, "Prue, can you hear me?"

She shut her eyes because the light, after all this gloom, was too bright. But she heard her own voice—so long silent—say, "Now I know. At last I know what it's all about."

"What are you talking about?" This time she heard the voice clearly, and it was harsh and loud with anxiety, and she recognized it. She opened her eyes again. The gray landscape had gone. Hanging above her in the clear daylight, looking enormous and alarmed, was Richard's face. She was back from wherever she had been, and she returned into the warmth and comfort bringing her great discovery with her. She smiled.

"What are you talking about?" said Richard again.

She drew a breath and began eagerly to tell him. But as she shaped the first sentence, she stopped. Her eyes, at first fixed on his face above, began to roam. They went from side to side, up and down. Then she said, "I don't know. I've forgotten." She closed her eyes again because the grayness of the recent country where she had made her discovery had turned into a headache. Grayness and headache; they seemed to be the same. Blackness and throbbing pain were the same, too. And this was another thing she had just discovered. Richard's voice, growing fainter and fainter—smaller and smaller—was saying, "Prue! Prue! Don't drift off again."

When she opened her eyes once more, she found that the familiar world had adjusted itself. It lay all about her. Sunlight; the sound of birds; treetops against the blue sky; strangely, a roof of rock above her and a rushing, roaring sound that she recognized.

"Water!" she screamed. "Richard. Quick! Water!" and sat up. Immediately her head seemed to split open, and the sunlight went black. She would have fallen backward if Richard's arm had not caught her in time, easing her on to the soft sand.

"It's all right," he said. "It's all right, Prue. We're safe. It's only the ordinary creek you can hear."

This time the blackness dispersed quite quickly. Her head still ached but bearably. She did not try to sit up again but asked, "What was it about the water? What was it that was so dreadful? I can't remember. Richard, what was it?" She saw him clearly now, kneeling beside her, trying to make her comfortable.

"Never mind about it now," he said. "I don't want you to worry about it. Just get better. We're quite safe."

"Get better?" she said. "I wasn't sick."

"No. Not sick," said Richard. "You had a crack on the head. Knocked you out. I'll tell you about it later. You must rest now, so you'll get stronger."

"I'm strong now," she said indignantly. Then she remembered what had happened when she had tried to sit up and became very quiet. She looked about her again and after a while said, "Wherever are we? This isn't a house. The roof's made of rock."

"It is rock," said Richard. "It's a cave. It's warm and dry and safe. Now rest, Prue, please."

She would have liked to ask why she had to rest in a cave by a creek and not in her own bed, but the effort of asking seemed monumental and she decided that later on would do for knowing. To show that she was willing to cooperate, even if strangely lazy, she smiled again at Richard even as her eyes closed. She felt herself sinking, deep and soft, into the familiar gray mists, and let herself fall, securely confident that this time there would be no more desolation. A watchman in her mind cried, "All's well," and her spark of life retreated deep inside her to burn with a small, quiet flame until more was demanded of it.

Twelve hours later she woke completely, rational, alert, and with only the smallest headache. The ache was localized now, and she put her hand up to her head. A great swelling just above the temple screamed silently as she pressed it. Her eyes flew open. Then she blinked and opened them again. A sudden, sharp fear clutched at the nerves in the very middle of her rib cage, for everything was black, and as her eyes were wide open, it seemed that the crack on her skull must have blinded her. Her hands, flaccid on the sand, slowly screwed themselves into fists as she clutched at her self-control. She had taken two long, tremulous breaths when something made her turn her head a fraction. A single bright pinpoint lit the blackness. She blinked quickly several times and then saw two more tiny gleaming holes in the canopy above. She held them with her eyes and dared not move again. As she waited, her ears, to which she had not been attending, directed a series of plangent sounds to her brain. Familiar sounds, lovely, homely sounds. And suddenly, in the darkness of the night she laughed aloud. "Frogs," she said clearly. "I can tell they're frogs."

Immediately there was a movement, a shuffling in the sand, and Richard's voice said out of the darkness, "Prue, are you all right?"

"Yes," she said. "Except for a bump I seem to have on my head. Richard, where are we? And why is it night?" She heard him move again and felt the warmth of his body beside her in the sand.

"You sound much better," he said. "I expect I can tell you now."

"Of course, you can tell me. I want to know where we are. This seems such a funny place to be—in the middle of the night." She stretched out her hand and felt him, warm and alive and very real. Then she took her hand back quickly and ran it down her own body. "We're *both* dressed," she said in a puzzled voice. "Go on, Richard. Tell me."

"Well—" He stopped, and she began to think he had decided to keep the extraordinary secret. Then he said, "Prue, how much do you remember?"

"What of? Richard, do go on."

"I mean, do you remember what happened when we were in the car?"

Suddenly she remembered, and after one short gasp, held her breath. "Yes," she said at last, and began to speak slowly and with many hesitations. "We were driving along. It was hot. It was very hot—and dusty. I was thirsty and Aunt Kate said we mustn't stop because we still had a long way to go. She asked you to give me an orange." She stopped, and after a few minutes' silence said, "Richard, where were we going?"

"To Adelaide. To the Festival," he said in a voice as quiet as her own.

"So we were. . . . And we'd been driving for hours—all the way from Sydney. Aunt Kate hadn't been able to leave till after lunch. We'd crossed the Blue

8

Mountains—I think. Anyway, we were on the western side of them. Coming down to the plains. And it was getting dark. Then clouds came, and we went through a storm. But it cleared and we went on. And it was getting dark." She seemed to be reciting, haltingly, a lesson learned long ago. "But we had to get to—somewhere— before we could stop, and we went on. And we came to this creek, and Aunt Kate said, 'It's only a little creek. It can't be very deep—' "

Her voice trailed off, and in the small silence the sound of the frogs came up from below, and the water made gurgling noises as it passed over pebbles. Suddenly she leaned over, clutching at Richard's coat. *"This* creek," she said loudly. "Richard, was it *this* creek?"

She felt him put his hand on her arm, patting and soothing. "Yes," he said. "It was this creek, but it's all right now. It's quite all right now."

"I remember," she said, and her voice was high and louder than necessary. "We had just begun to go down the concrete dip where the water crossed the road at a ford, and it was dark and Aunt Kate was still saying it couldn't be very deep, and then she said, 'What's that funny noise? Is it thunder?' And it got louder and louder and something came out of the dark and hit the car and the car went sideways, and—" For a long time there was silence, and then she said very quietly, "I don't remember any more. What happened, Richard?"

This time he moved quite close to her and put his arm around her shoulders. The warmth was comforting and the support was reassuring. "It must have been a snap flood—after the storm," he said. "Somewhere upstream from us. That storm must have been savage somewhere

9

else and the rain must have pelted down. Before we had time to do anything the flood picked up the car and swept it off the road. I think we turned over several times. We had no time to do anything—open the door, even. Then we stopped rolling, and I think we must have got wedged on the bottom against a rock or something. And the water started to come in. I can't—I don't—" For the first time he seemed to find it hard to make the words come. He swallowed and then went on, "I'm not at all clear—it was such a mess, and everybody was all over the place. I didn't even know which was right side up. I think I took my shoe off and broke a window with it. At any rate I've lost one shoe and gashed my arm. I think I pushed someone through the window. It must have been you. And I couldn't—I couldn't—reach anyone else. I felt about. I tried. I know I tried." Prue failed to recognize the jagged voice as Richard's. But now it stopped dead. It was a long time before he said very quietly, "Anyway, I remember getting out of the window myself. I had to, Prue. By then the car was full of water, and I had to take a breath. Or drown. I wouldn't have been much help drowned, would I?" She recognized the anguish in his voice and for a moment became Richard trapped in the car, lungs bursting, and knowing there were two others whom he could not reach and whose lungs were bursting, too.

"Naturally you had to get out. Go on, Richard."

The calm acceptance in her tone must have reassured him, for he went on more calmly, "As soon as I was out, I got swept away by the current. I remember getting banged about on the stones. And then after—oh, hours—I suppose not more than a few minutes, I somehow got stuck in the shallows. As soon as I realized I wasn't going on with the current, I rolled quickly a couple of times to get clear of the beastly water. When I knew I was on dry land, I must have blacked out, because I don't remember anything more until I woke up with the sun on me."

"And—where had I got to?" asked Prue.

"That was the funny thing. You were lying on this bit of a sandbank right beside me. But there was blood on your face, and—I thought you were dead."

"Goodness!" said Prue, and rubbed her cheek with the palm of her hand. "It doesn't feel bloody now."

"No. I washed the blood off it when I found you were still breathing." She felt the muscles of his arm tighten for a moment on her shoulder. "Gosh, I was glad when I saw you were breathing."

"And what happened to Aunt Kate? And Peter. Where's Peter, Richard?"

It was a long time before he said, "That's the trouble. I don't know. I haven't seen any sign of them."

Prue said in a sharp voice, "Didn't you go back to the car? How long have we been here? Haven't you looked?"

"Of course I've looked. My own mother."

"And Peter's my brother, and I'll have to find him. I'll go back to the car as soon as it's light."

"You can't," said Richard, and his voice was tired. "Don't you think I've tried? There's a damned great cliff we must have got swept over. I expect that's how you got that bump on your head. I couldn't get back up it. I tried. And I didn't dare leave you long enough to try going around. It would have taken I don't know how long, and even then I mightn't have made it. Wait till you see this country in the daylight."

"How long, Richard?" said Prue, and the anger had

died out of her voice. "How long have we been here?"

"Two days," he said. "I began to think you'd never come round. I knew I'd never get you out of here on my own. I was nearly going crazy. Prue, you've no idea how horrible it is here. Even now I don't know how we'll make it."

She was silent, oppressed by the weight of his hopelessness. If Richard had no answer, there probably wasn't one. At last she said, "Two days. Two whole days. What did you have to eat?"

He gave a kind of laugh. "I couldn't find a restaurant, so, naturally, there haven't been any meals."

It seemed a rebuke for a foolish question, but she said, "I only thought you might have found something—a fish, or a nut, or something like that."

"In this place? Three course meals don't grow on trees." He swallowed, as if the thought of a three course meal were more than he could bear.

"I'm sorry," she said. "Naturally you must have looked. What a mercy there's water. Wait a minute." She stopped, and he felt her wriggling. Then she grunted with satisfaction, and he felt something being pressed into his hand. "There," she said. "I knew I had some."

The small objects in his palm felt leathery. "What's this?" he asked.

"Dried apricots. We had them in the car, remember? Go on, Richard. Eat them."

He gave a gasp, which was chopped off short as he crammed the apricots into his mouth. She could hear him chewing as if his jaw muscles had been starved, not only of food, but of exercise, too. The saliva began to flow, and he was swallowing as he chewed. At last he stopped. "To think," he said, when he had swallowed for the last time, "that I could have spent my life eating dried apricots—any time I liked to buy a pound or so, and I never knew how gorgeous they were."

"I told you they were nice," said Prue.

She felt him move suddenly, and he said "Prue!"

"What's the matter? What's wrong?" The tone had meant something serious.

"I've eaten them. I've eaten them all, Prue."

"It's all right," she said soothingly. "They weren't poisoned."

"I know. But they were yours. And I've eaten them—all."

She had not thought, ten minutes ago, that she would be laughing for a long time, but she laughed now. "That's what I gave them to you for. I meant you to eat them. You said you were hungry."

"But they were yours. And you must be hungry. I never thought. Oh, Prue, I am sorry."

"I'm not hungry, and I wanted you to eat them. I *gave* them to you. Don't be silly."

"They were probably the last food we shall have till we get out of here—if we get out of here," he said. "And I've gone and eaten the lot."

"So long as they did you good," said Prue. "And I'm sure we'll find something to eat. Everything else does."

"Everything else eats grubs and grass. I'll starve before I'll do that." A certain resentfulness had crept into his tone. Perhaps he realized it, for he said now more cheerfully, "Whatever happens, we can't do anything till daylight, and you should rest again. Let's try to sleep till the sun comes up."

"Yes," she said. "I'll have to get stronger." He removed his arm from her shoulders, and she lay back. She

13

could hear him doing the same. Then she heard him give a long sigh. "Richard," she said quietly.

"Yes, Prue?"

"I shall have to try to go back."

"It's no use. You won't be able to."

"I'll have to try, just the same. I expect I won't be able to—specially if you couldn't. But I have to try—myself."

"Very well. In the morning."

She could feel that he was lying on his back, and she caught the gleam of his open eyes. After a long silence she said, "Do you think we'll find them? Aunt Kate and Peter? Do you think they could have got out? Could they have got through after you?"

"I hope so. Oh, Prue, I hope so." She heard him turn quickly on his side and his back was toward her. The frogs croaked on and the water splashed over the pebbles. Overhead the pinpricks of light had moved, as the earth left them behind, rolling on toward the waiting sun and the new day.

[2]

Prue woke from a dream of anxious hurrying to find the cave full of noise and movement. It was daylight, but a colorless, sunless daylight full of dust particles and flying twigs and leaves. Without thinking, she sat bolt upright and felt for a moment the black dizziness of her first attempt to sit up. She screwed up her eyes and, stiffening her arms behind her, leaned on her fists. Gradually the dizziness passed, and she opened her eyes again. It was wind that filled the cave with wailing and dust and almost drowned the sound of the creek below. It rushed in from across the gully, hit the wall behind her, bellowed with fury, and swirled out again, taking handfuls of the dry sand at the back of the cave with it. The particles were encrusted around the corners of her eyes. She pulled a handkerchief from her pocket and wiped them. Then, for the first time, she took notice of what was outside the cave. Below, at the bottom of a short slope, the creek came swirling around a big rock, lapping the edge of a patch of sand at the foot of the slope. Just out of reach of the water, the sand was strewn and heaped with debris —flotsam that had been flung there by the current, just as she and Richard must have been flung there when the creek came down in spate two days before.

There were tumbled rocks along its bed, gleaming black and wet as the water boiled its way through them. It was impossible to see upstream beyond the rock, and she could only guess that around the bend, out of sight, were more and bigger rocks. Downstream to her right the current seemed to lose a little of its force, the jumble of rocks looked slightly less formidable, and the creek bed wider. By the time the creek took its next turn, the slope on either side had become less steep as if, much farther downstream, the land could be flattening out. Across the creek facing her, the trees that clung to the slope were doing a mad dance in the wind. Like a ragged *corps de ballet,* they bowed together, first to the right, then to the left, and then as a different draft of air took them, twirled in a frenzy on their stems so that the leaves showed alternate silver and gray-green. And as they danced, the trees hissed and rattled, shuddered and roared, and showers of dead leaves and pieces of bark flew from them in all directions. It was as if the whole

15

slope were in motion and howling protest.

Overhead, as she peered up from the mouth of the cave, she could see that the sky was white and colorless, though the glare of sunlight was painful. After the benign peace of yesterday and the calm of the night, the elements had begun to snarl. It was a time to close the gates, to be watchful and beware. It was as well she felt better, for this was no day for resting.

She looked down at Richard, still sleeping on the sand beside her. It was surprising that in this hubbub he still slept, but perhaps after his two nights of vigil, waiting for her to become conscious, he was taking the sleep he needed. But the wind must have penetrated his dreams, for it was not a peaceful sleep. There were unrelaxed lines between his eyes, and his lips kept moving as if he tried to speak. Now and then, beneath the olive green shirt, his body twitched. His cheeks were sunken and putty-colored in the cruel light.

He had always stood, in her eyes, for everything that was excellent and admirable. She had known him and his mother for as long as she could remember. Aunt Kate was her mother's favorite, though distant, cousin. Because she had lost her engineer husband in a dramatic and tragic mine accident a long time ago she had always carried about her, for Prue, an aura of something special —something that was more like the stories she read than the sort of humdrum suburban life that Prue led with her own family. And a little of this had fallen on Richard, too. They lived in the middle of Sydney in a flat high up in a tall building that to Prue's eyes was perfect. It was often full of Richard's glamorous friends or of Aunt Kate's equally glamorous but older friends. And Richard had sailed gloriously through school, until now, with honors for scholarship and sport all about him, he was poised on the brink of university life. Prue's mother said he was a credit to Aunt Kate, who had, single-handed, brought him up to be what he was.

For Richard was always busy, always in a hurry, with a hundred friends and a hundred interests. He knew every inch of the city and could—and often did—take Prue, who was nervous of being alone in town, anywhere she needed to go. She saw him always as poised, confident, superb in the middle of the surge and press of city life.

Her own life seemed in contrast slow and uneventful. Prue and her brother Peter lived and went to school on the very outside edge of the city where they could see the open country not far away. In spite of the fact that their father went to the city every day to work, the basis of their lives had always been different.

Peter was happiest left to himself outside in their garden or in one of the vacant allotments or, more usually, by the little creek that ran through a patch of scrub at the bottom of the garden. Prue, halfway between the ages of Richard and Peter, could never decide which of them she liked being with best. She was thrilled when Richard included her in any of his plans, but she could be completely happy catching yabbies in the creek with Peter, too.

They had never been able to persuade Richard to take the smallest interest in these activities of Peter's on the occasions when he came to visit them. They realized humbly that these were childish pleasures not worthy of Richard's advanced age and intellect. Aunt Kate sometimes laughed and said Richard would never be able to grow so much as a cabbage, because earth was something he never touched. When she said this, Prue would look at her own begrimed fingers and stuff them into her pockets. She was ashamed of not having noticed how dirty they were. Peter never cared. As with other small boys, mud and dust were a part of his life and were washed off him only under protest.

That Richard, in spite of their shortcomings, was never-failingly kind to his cousins was a recurring wonder to them both. They had always had for him a respectful devotion fed by admiration and restrained by awe. Finding Richard beside her when she woke in the cave had given Prue an immediate confidence that soon all would be well. Sooner or later Richard would find Peter and Aunt Kate and get her home.

Looking at his face now, undefended and with the first few tentative whiskers about the chin, she felt a sudden foreboding. If he had lost his mother now, if Aunt Kate had not found her way out of the car, he would be left quite alone. For the first time in her life the awe Prue felt for him was melted in a rush of pity. Then she remembered that he was Richard after all, and Aunt Kate could still be all right, and Richard would always find a way. Richard would never be beaten. She was thankful that he was there beside her, but there seemed no point in waking him, so she sat with her legs drawn up and clasped by her arms, rested her chin on her knees, and considered the prospect that faced them.

Two things filled her mind. They must get back to the car to find out about Aunt Kate and Peter if they could, and they must get to somewhere where there was food.

The sooner they did both, the better. She put her hand to her head. The bump had subsided, although it was still there. She wondered if she would be able to stand, glanced once more at Richard, and decided to try. She crept on all fours to the mouth of the cave and, holding onto the rocky wall, pulled herself upright. Her legs seemed prepared to hold her, though she had a mild sensation of floating. She had moved along the ledge to the right of the cave when she heard Richard shout. Before she could move, he appeared at the mouth of the cave. He must have woken abruptly, for he tottered a little, hanging out over the slope to the creek. Then he grasped the rock and steadied himself. His eyes searched the length of the creek below.

"It's all right, Richard. I'm here," said Prue.

He swung around and saw her standing on the shelf beside him, her brown hair windblown, her jeans still covered with sand from the floor of the cave. She swayed in the wind, and he put out a hand to support her, even as he shouted furiously, "What on earth do you think you're doing?"

"I was seeing if I could stand, and I can. Did I frighten you, Richard?"

"I thought you'd fallen into the creek. You should never have gone without waking me. You're a stupid little girl." He pulled her back more roughly than he meant, and she stumbled against him, clutching at his shirt. She was very light and easy to support. He was remorseful at once. "I'm sorry, Prue. I didn't mean— how do you feel? How is your head?" He peered into her face.

"I'm better. And I didn't want to wake you. I wasn't

19

going anywhere. Just trying my legs. And I'm not little."

"No. Well, never mind. Come into the cave out of the wind." He pulled her toward it, but to his surprise she resisted him.

"I'm not going back to the cave. I don't have to, and we must get moving. You do see, don't you?" She peered into his face, and until he looked into hers, he thought she was pleading. Then he saw that she was not; she was merely making him believe he could not stop her now.

"Do you feel well enough?" he said. "It's a dreadful day for climbing about."

"We can't wait any longer, and I feel well enough." She put her hand in his, but it was not for support; it was to lead him down toward the creek.

They left their cave, the sand still flattened from the weight of their bodies for two days and nights, and went down to the water. When they had drunk, they turned upstream toward the big rock that altered its course and hid its upper reaches from view. Richard tried once to stop her, saying that there was no point in tiring themselves to find out again what he had already found out once—that there was no way out in that direction. But she ignored him and went on. Once or twice she stumbled, but she seemed to gain strength as she went on, trudging through the soft sand, slipping over wet rocks, clutching at branches and saplings that edged the creek. The big rock forced them into the water as they rounded the bend. Now they saw a wall of glistening rock, wet and smooth, right in front of them. The water, snatched by the wind as it curved over the shelf above, sprayed out in a veil of iridescent drops over the rocks below. The fall was not great, but the wall was sheer and quite obviously unclimbable. Prue looked to the right and left, but she knew she was beaten. There was no way, even for a light body like hers.

"You see?" said Richard quietly behind her.

She turned. "How did we ever survive?" she asked him. "Why weren't we killed when we came over, if that's where we came?"

"There's a little pool that the water normally falls into. It's hidden by the rock in front of us, and the wind's stopping the water falling straight today, but we would have fallen into that. How we weren't killed bouncing over the rocks afterward, I have no idea. You nearly were."

She nodded slowly. Then she turned around, and he saw that her face was grave. "Did you look among the rocks? If—if—Aunt Kate or Peter had come over they could be—they might be still somewhere among these rocks."

"They're not," Richard said quickly. "You must believe me, Prue. They're not. I looked everywhere. I didn't want to find them—like that. But I looked everywhere. They are not here."

"Then we must go on. Down the creek until we find a way out." She went past him with her head bent, watching the ground at her feet, and scarcely noticed when he turned and followed her. When she reached the patch of sand, she stopped again, looking up at the slopes of the gorge. The wind wrapped a strand of hair around her throat and blew a tangled bundle of flotsam about her feet. She looked up at the slopes on either side.

"It's no good," said Richard. "It gets steep near the top. You see, I tried everywhere about here, within sight

21

of the cave. We shall have to go on down."

This time she accepted his decision and moved to go forward, but the flotsam caught at her ankle, and she stumbled. She felt Richard's hand at her elbow and heard him say, "Here, hold on while I get you out of all this rubbish." He bent down in front of her, pulling at the weed and twigs. She heard him give a grunt of surprise, and he stood up with something that looked familiar in his hand.

"My shoe! The one I took off to break the car window." He sat down to put it on. He shook out the gravel and eased it onto his foot. "It'll do. It'll warm up in a minute. Now I can go anywhere. Come on, Prue."

He strode off and she followed. She had to concentrate on keeping up, controlling her occasional plunges into dizziness. It was hard to say whether they were caused by the bump on her head or by hunger. If it was hunger, he was probably feeling dizzy too. No point in mentioning something that could be overcome and could not be helped.

They walked on downstream, and the wind buffeted them and howled, and the trees danced their mad dance and hissed and showered them with leaves as they passed. Every now and then they stopped to drink, for the dry wind sucked the moisture from their bodies. For a long time they did not speak but picked their way on, crossing the creek when they had to. Richard complained at first, saying that wet shoes lost their shape and gave you blisters, but there is no point in saying the same thing every time you step into a puddle, and in the end he fell silent.

Their progress was very slow. Mostly their eyes were

22

on the ground, but from time to time Prue looked up to see where he was leading her. Always he seemed to be engaged in a personal battle with the wind, or with whatever lay beneath his feet. A gust would catch him just as he was off balance, so that he waved his arms and staggered, or a stone would roll as he put his weight on it, or his shoe would slip off, and he would have to stop and put it on again. His way forward appeared to her as a series of encounters with one or another of many hostile forces and each step onward was a kind of victory. His clothes, the fashionable high-necked shirt and the white moleskin pants, which had so impressed her when they began their trip to Adelaide, were bedraggled now with sweat and dirt. The moleskins had lost their creases in the plunge down the creek and clung around his buttocks like a half-sloughed skin. The shirt hugged his shoulders, creasing under the armpits, and every so often he ran a finger around the inside of the collar as if it were strangling him. But he fought his way on, and she followed.

It was a long time before Prue understood that Richard was doing the best he could in an environment that was totally strange to him. He was the leader and he led, and she followed because she had always done so. She did not know and could not have guessed that he was feeling bewildered and inadequate. For once, the situation was beyond him. For her sake, he was doing his best not to let her know this. There came a time when her feelings ceased to matter to him, so chaotic were his own. But this was not yet.

After a particularly difficult patch, Richard stopped and looked around. Perhaps he saw the pallor of Prue's face or the droop of her shoulders, for he said, "We'll

23

have a rest here. Let's sit down."

They found a flat rock in the shade of an overhanging tree and sat, panting. When he had got his breath back, he said, "Can you manage, do you think? We ought to be able to leave the creek and make our way back soon."

"I can manage. I'm not even very hungry."

Richard made a sound that was meant to be a laugh. "I wish I wasn't. I'm so hungry I could eat pretty well anything—raw."

She put her hand on his forearm. "Poor Richard. Should we stop and look for something to eat? There must be something . . ." Her voice trailed off.

"I'd rather not waste time. While we can keep going—unless you can't, Prue?" His tone, urgent and raw, reminded her that they had a more serious cause for distress than hunger.

"Someone must have rescued them by now, mustn't they? Mustn't they, Richard? It's more than two days. Someone must have." Her voice stopped, and the high sound was whipped away by the wind.

"Yes, of course." He got up abruptly. "Come on, Prue."

It was around the next bend of the creek that they found him. They had been going to tackle the slope because it looked more possible here, and they had taken their first steps uphill when Prue looked down onto a grassy bank a short way beyond where they had left the creek. At first she thought it was simply another bundle of flotsam—strange souvenirs collected by the stream on its way to the sea and dropped in a convenient eddy as a small child drops a toy. But this bundle seemed to be made of rags, and she stopped and looked more carefully. There was more than rags. "Richard!" she screamed, and he swung round.

It was a high, shrill scream, and even through the howling of the wind, it carried as far as the grassy bank—as far as the bundle of rags. The rags immediately became convulsed, swirled about, and transformed themselves into a small boy in the act of scrambling to his feet. He looked about wildly, still half asleep, and then saw the two figures on the slope.

But Prue had seen him first, and now she cried, "Peter!" and rushed toward him, her hands held out.

[3]

H IS FACE LIT UP, and he ran to meet her. He shouted as he ran, "Where you been all the time? I looked for you."

Prue felt him carefully all over, as if doubting his physical presence, and it was Richard who said, "Where have *you* been, you mean? What are you doing here?"

Peter said, "Ouch!" as his sister found a bruise and then looked up at Richard. "I came down with the creek. Didn't you?" Then he said, "Ouch!" again.

"Richard says he and I were washed onto the same patch of sand," said Prue. "Wasn't it lucky?"

"If the creek washed you as far as this," said Richard, "I can't imagine why you weren't drowned or battered to bits."

"I *am* battered to bits," said Peter. "Nearly. And I would have drowned if I hadn't swum."

"Swum? You never swam all this way?" Richard's voice suggested he must be deliberately holding something back.

But Prue said, "He's a good swimmer, Richard, for his size. He probably did." She was feeling more gently now, for his small body did seem to be a mass of bruises and grazes. So far the bones appeared to be holding together.

"I swum," said Peter. "But the creek brought me this far. I swum so I could keep my head up and breathe."

"I can't understand how he came so far though," said Prue. She sat back on her haunches, satisfied he had suffered only superficial damage.

"More bouyant than we are," said Richard. "That's why."

Prue gazed at her seven-year-old brother, drinking him in from head to foot—the tousled brown hair, the alert, narrow face badly scratched just now, the matchstick arms and legs not yet grown into elbow and knee joints, the torn, washed-out blue jeans and tattered T-shirt—and suddenly she leaned forward and flung her arms around him, squeezing until he grunted.

"Ouch!" she heard him say loudly. She felt herself grow hot and begin to sweat, and then a black cloud descended from the sky, enveloping her completely. She opened her eyes to find herself sitting on the grass, propped up by Richard, while Peter, looking appalled, splashed water from his cupped hands into her face.

"That'll do, Peter," came Richard's voice behind her. "She's coming around now."

Her head had begun to ache fiercely, but she managed to smile. "Oh, Peter," she said, and put out her hand to touch him again.

Richard, who liked everything to be clear-cut, with no

untidy ends, now tried to find out what Peter had been doing for the past two and a half days. Why had he not gone on or back or somewhere else? What, if anything, had he had to eat? What had he intended to do if they had not turned up? To most of these questions Peter gave vague answers. He did not know how the time had passed, except that by the time he had been tossed up on the grass by the creek he had been terribly tired, and when he woke after a sleep that could have been long or short, he had been so stiff and sore that he had not bothered to move for some time. He had not really thought about food, except that, now he remembered, he had chewed a bit of grass or something, and he thought he remembered trying a grub because he knew Aborigines ate them. It had not been specially nice, but it had stopped him wanting to eat for a bit. Yes, he expected he'd been having a little sleep when they found him, 'cos he was somehow tired. But he had intended moving on. On? Well, down the creek till he came to something or someone.

Then, more urgently, Richard asked him if he remembered how he had got out of the car. Had he and his Aunt Kate got out the same way? After this question there was utter silence. Peter frowned, sighed deeply once or twice, scratched the ground with his finger, and at last looked up. "I don't remember," he said.

"Think," said Richard.

So he thought again while they waited. Then he said, "I don't like remembering much."

Prue leaned toward him. "Please try, Peter. You see we don't know what happened to Aunt Kate. Richard has to know."

Peter's eyes flashed once to Richard's face and fell

again. He began to speak slowly. "See, I don't know properly what happened. Everyone was all over the place. And the water—" He shivered. "There was a little corner where there was air. Then Richard's legs went up in the air through the roof."

"That was the window," said Richard. "I broke it. Prue and I got out that way."

"I went up after your legs," said Peter. He stopped and then said in a perplexed way, "You only had one shoe on. Those good new shoes. They *were* nice, Richard."

"Go *on,* Peter," said Prue.

"I went up after the feet, and then the water sort of swished me about."

"But Aunt Kate," said Prue. "Can you remember if Aunt Kate was still in the car?"

The effort of recollection screwed Peter's face into a scowl. He knew now why his memory mattered so much, and he was trying very hard. Then the scowl left his face, and it became distressed. "I didn't look," he said desperately. "I didn't look, Richard, but the car was much more empty. More empty," he repeated, "except for all the water," and could tell them nothing more. Like theirs, his mind was full of confused images all tinged with the horror of a nightmare. And, like them, the idea of escape had been all that he had thought of.

"She couldn't have got out first, do you think?" said Prue.

Richard lifted his head slowly. He seemed to be looking at the trees that still waved on the far side of the creek. But he was seeing the inside of the car. "She could have," he said at last. "She could have, and she might have. But I am afraid—somehow—I don't think she did."

28

After a long silence while each of them found important things to do with their fingers, like separating strands of grass or poking pieces of stick into the ground, Peter said in a brighter tone, "Well, anyway, Richard, if she got out, she'll be all right now, 'cos she hasn't come down the creek, has she? And if she didn't—" He stopped, finding he had got himself into a disastrous position. But something had to be said, so he ended a little wildly, "—if she didn't, there's no need to worry any more now." It was meant to be helpful, but it left a painful vacuum among the three of them.

At last Richard got to his feet. "Peter's right," he said in a matter-of-fact tone that Prue knew was false. "It's too late to worry. It's decided now—one way or the other. We needn't hurry specially, except to find a house and a telephone and some food."

"Down the creek's best," said Peter. "There's sure to be a house soon."

They never afterward knew why they allowed Peter's decision to stand. At the time neither Richard nor Prue thought of querying it. They left the patch of grass, turned their backs on the place they had come from, and with united purpose began to make their way downstream.

They always remembered quite clearly the next two days of walking. The creek they followed, the country they passed through, the air, the wind, the sky above, all were normal—the kind of things they were accustomed to. Sometimes the wind blew as on the day they began, and sometimes it dropped and there was calm. Mostly the sky was clear and blue, and the sun shone down warm and pleasant, but not yet too hot. The trees, the birds, the busy insects and the grass beneath their feet were all as they expected. That they failed to find the house they were looking for or a single telephone line or a road was unfortunate and uncomfortable for them, but it was not unusual. Richard agreed with Peter and kept repeating, as each bend of the creek revealed another stretch of country empty of houses or human habitation of any kind, that they had only to follow the water and sooner or later they must come to someone's homestead. Water, particularly in Australia, was not a commodity usually disregarded by men. So he encouraged them. Prue, with a headache that kept recurring so that she seemed to walk in a dream, needed all the encouragement he could give her. He was Richard and he knew what he was doing, and she could rely on him to lead her eventually home. Her trust in him kept her putting one foot before the other.

Mercifully, they had the creek to drink from, but their hunger grew ravenous and demanding. It forced them often to stop and consider ways of satisfying it. Usually it was Peter who found the answer. Unlike Richard, he never worried about where the food was to come from, but it was he who found it in the end. Perhaps this was because he looked for it in places Richard never thought of looking. At one time he found a plover's nest in the grass, and they took all the eggs but one while the plover was elsewhere and ate them. Another time he saw a rabbit hole in a bank and dug it out, finding a grown rabbit and six young ones. They were not country children, and Richard and Prue shrank from the killing, but Peter, who did not know the countryman's way of quickly and painlessly snapping the neck, discovered his own method and despatched them all with a quick swing against a rock. When Richard said, "I don't know how you can," he looked at him in surprise and replied, "But we need them. We have to eat."

They were trying to face the thought of eating them raw when Richard said, "Hey, wait a minute," and began feeling in his pockets. At the third pocket he said, "Ah," and produced a cigarette lighter.

"Didn't know you carried one of those," said Peter. "Didn't know you smoked."

"I don't. But it often comes in handy. It's an old one of Mum's." It was the first time he had mentioned his mother for some time, and for a while it reduced them all to silence. This was broken eventually by Peter, who had been collecting dry grass and sticks.

"You could light it now, Richard," he said, "if it still works after the water."

To their joy it worked at the third flick, and they were all enormously cheered by the sight of their own little fire. They more or less skinned the rabbits with Peter's pocket knife, and if this first meal was not as nice as some they cooked later, it taught them that it is best to remove the intestines before cooking meat over a fire.

As they walked on, the country, as Richard had predicted, became flatter. The creek bed grew wider and the slopes on either side less steep. The thick, scrubby eucalypts that had covered them at first gave way to grass and clumps of briar rose. And instead of the eucalypts, casuarinas grew along the banks, near enough to the creek to feel the water with their roots. In the daytime the air was full of the song of thrushes, the warbling of magpies, and the excited chirrup of flycatchers. Bright green grass parrots flew up in little flocks in front of their feet, and gray and white galahs swung on the branches and peered down at them. Now and then one or two white sulphur-crested cockatoos shrieked in the sky above. From time to time they surprised wild duck—wood duck, black duck, and an occasional shag—and these would fly, quacking, downstream until they came upon them again, and then they would swirl indignantly up from the water and fly back to where they had come from. Sometimes, when the creek ran dark and quiet under the trees, the snout of a water rat would make a silent, spreading triangle of ripples in the water as he headed for the farther bank. But they never saw a house or a telephone line, and it was Peter who pointed out, when the creek banks had quite flattened out, that there were no fences either.

Each night they found a dry and sheltered spot, under an overhanging bank or among the spreading roots of a casuarina and lay down to sleep. And during this time the weather remained warm and dry, and after the first day's wind had dropped, it seemed to them that there was little to fear in living under the open sky. It came, in fact, as a kind of revelation. Even Prue and Peter, living so near the countryside, had never slept under the open sky. Their holidays had always been by the surf in a rented cottage. As for Richard, it was not a form of entertainment that would ever have entered his mind. Never before had any of them met conditions in the least like these. They began, tentatively, to enjoy the open life and the freedom.

It was on the third day, when they had come out from among the hills and the country stretched all around them, wide, flat, and bare of everything but the covering grass and occasional clumps of trees, and the sky had grown enormous above, that Richard said, "I always thought creeks were supposed to grow bigger the farther you went downstream."

"So they do," said Prue.

"Well, this one's getting smaller."

It was true. Now that they all looked carefully, they could see that there was far less water passing between the banks than there had been. There was not enough to rush and bubble now. The water was still there, but it flowed smooth and placid and unhurried over or around the stones in its path. It was dwindling.

"What if it stops?" said Peter.

But now their bodies told them they had passed the point of no return. They could not go all the long way back. They were committed, and they must go on. Richard still said they would find a house soon.

[4]

THEY WALKED ON, and the creek wound its sluggish way through an undulating plain. Later they remembered that there had been cattle scattered on it, feeding. There were muddy cattle tracks in places along the creek, and twice they came upon groups of wild-looking cows with half-grown calves that threw up their heads at the sight of them and took off, tails high, out across the plain.

"Not used to us having two legs, I 'spect," said Peter.

"But it means there must be somebody who owns them," said Richard. "We can't be too far off now."

All morning they walked across the open plain, and the wind dropped again. The sun became hotter as mid-day approached, and insects and flies rose up from the semi-stagnant pools of the creek. They stopped often to drink, too thirsty to worry whether the water was flowing cleanly. In their increasing thirst they forgot they were hungry. About noon, when the sun was overhead, the ground started to shimmer in the heat. They began to imagine wide pools—even lakes—with trees reflected in them. Prue, who was walking in her usual half dream, fighting off the recurring headache, looked up once and said, "Look at those hills right in front."

"Those aren't real hills," said Richard. "They're a kind of illusion caused by the heat haze. Real hills would never be as blue as that. I don't think it's even clouds."

"I thought it was hills," said Prue, "sticking up against the horizon. My seeing must have gone funny."

"You look, Peter," said Richard.

But Peter had been helping a small green frog to swim to the side of a pool and could not be persuaded to give an opinion. He squatted by the frog, watching it scramble out on its long legs into the grass. After its swim it seemed happy to sit down, but it gazed at him out of bulging eyes, the pulse in its little throat going in and out. "They say you can eat frogs' legs," he said as he got up.

Several times they sat down in the grass to rest. But there was no point in stopping at lunchtime because there was no lunch. Mainly, they trudged on through the hot afternoon, watching their creek grow smaller and the grass on the plain become longer and more tussocky. The creek went on, squashy and muddy between the tussocks, and the ground round about became springy and moist. At about three-thirty Richard stopped and said, "Which way do we go now? Can anyone see the creek?"

"It's gone," said Peter. "It went a little way back there. I wondered when you'd notice. It's just bog everywhere now."

Prue came out of her dream, shaken by a sudden apprehension. As usual, she looked to Richard. But he was saying in an angry voice to Peter, "Well, you might have told me."

"Why?" said Peter.

"Because I would have—" He stopped, for there was nothing different that he would have done, and he knew it. They could not go back. One way was the same as another, and wherever they were going, they must get there fast, for now they had neither food nor water.

"What shall we do, Richard?" said Prue. She could suddenly see them—three small and helpless people in a vast and empty plain, covered by a remote and even vaster sky, and there was nothing and no one to know or care that they existed. The feeling was an ache of desolation that was faintly familiar. A cool breeze crept out of somewhere and curled around her ears.

"We must go on," said Richard.

"Where to—on?" said Peter. "Do you still know where we've come from?" They had turned around several times while they had been looking for the creek. One way in this marshy flat was the same as another.

"Yes, of course. I—" said Richard, turning around rapidly once or twice. "No," he said at last, and sat down.

Prue sat beside him, glad of the excuse to rest. Only

Peter, untiring, hopped from tussock to tussock and said, "Now what, Richard? Now what?"

"I must think," said Richard, and for the first time the confidence had seeped out of his voice.

Prue lay back and closed her eyes. The little breeze still cooled her face, and she was grateful. The sound of humming insects rose up around her, interrupted now and then by the heavy buzz of a passing blowfly. One or two frogs croaked in the mud among the tussocks, high above a floating kestrel gave his shrill ki-ki-ki, and far away a high bugling note told her a cow had mislaid her calf. The smell of damp earth and dry grass floated to her nostrils on the little breeze. Her relaxing body tingled. Hopeful? Suspicious? She could not be sure, but it was beginning to feel something that her mind did not yet know. It was as if she floated in suspense until some resolution should be made, but she did not know when or where it would be made or who would make it. Somewhere in this loneliness was reassurance, but she could not tell where. After a while she stood up, and at last she spoke.

"I can still see those hills, Richard."

"Where? Show me." Richard got up at once.

"There." She pointed in the direction of the sun, which was sliding down the sky and was now halfway to the horizon. "There's a sort of haze in front of them, and the sun's been in our eyes, so we couldn't see properly. But they're there. And that's the west."

"Then that's where we'll go." Richard's voice was confident again. "We'll walk toward them while we can still see. Then we'll rest, and we'll walk again as soon as it's light."

36

"Yes," said Prue meekly. It was comfortable to be guided by Richard, not to have to make up her own mind. But Peter said, "Why? Why there, Richard?"

Richard was striding ahead and did not hear, or perhaps he did not wish to say only, "It's something to aim at."

That night they ate the frogs' legs. Peter caught the frogs, Prue collected the dry grass for the fire, and Richard lit it and did his best to cook the slippery, flabby little things that Peter handed to him. With the cool of the evening their hunger had returned, but the fire produced more smoke than heat, and the frogs' legs, perhaps because they were more smoked than cooked, tasted very peculiar. They ate them somehow, and afterward Richard went off and was sick.

"Pity to waste them," said Peter when he returned. "They were almost nice, weren't they?"

The water that they found by digging a hole in the mud was almost as peculiar as the frogs' legs, but they drank it, and it quenched the worst of their thirst and helped them to forget the frogs' legs.

They woke in the cold, pre-dawn hush all suffering from stomach cramps and did not know if they were caused by hunger or by what they had absorbed the night before. Their clothes were damp and their joints were stiff, but as soon as they caught their first glimpse of the hills—a pencil line on the faintly luminous horizon— they went on. That day as they walked, they were aware that the weather was changing. Subtle alterations were taking place in the sky and in the air about them. The rustle of the grass in the tussocks changed its note, and out on the plain the cows began to move off all in one direction until they became no more than dots on the horizon. One blink, and they were gone. This seemed the sundering of their last link with humankind.

As the day wore on, the blue color bleached out of the sky, and the sun burned more strongly behind a thin film of cloud. There were no kestrels in the sky now, and the frogs had stopped croaking. It was an empty and a waiting land they walked through. But the hills were growing bigger. They loomed quite high—blue and dark—and for no clear reason they held a promise of rescue.

This was how it seemed to Prue on that last ordinary afternoon, and the word "rescue" floating through her mind started a train of thought that made her say to Richard, "Don't you think someone will be looking for us by now?"

He stopped at once. "Of course they will. Of course. I never thought, but of course they will be looking for us." Vitality poured into him.

"Where?" said Peter.

"What do you mean—where?"

"Where will they look? This is a funny kind of place to find someone that got washed off a road in a car. That's what I mean."

"Well," said Richard robustly, "when they've looked in all the likely places they'll have to start looking in the unlikely places, won't they?"

"Hm," said Peter, and pounced on a grasshopper and stuffed it into his mouth. He chewed and after a moment, spat it out. "Nearly all prickles," he said indignantly.

Richard had hurriedly turned away and now he set off again.

The thought of rescue haunted them all the rest of the afternoon, and just before dark, as if conjured out of their passionate wishes, the very faint sound of an aeroplane floated down from the sky. It grew louder, and they stopped and caught their breath. In that huge and colorless expanse above, it was hard to say where the sound was coming from.

"Jets are never where their sound is," said Peter. "I look, but I never see them where I think they are."

"This isn't a jet," said Richard. "It's something smaller. And it might be looking for us."

"Perhaps we should do something to attract its attention," said Prue. "Wave our arms, or something."

Richard laughed shortly. "If you waved anything it'd have to be a lot bigger than an arm—something like a huge piece of colored plastic."

"But we haven't got any," said Prue.

Then Peter said, "I see it. Way over there. Teeny." He pointed in a vague easterly direction. "Getting littler," he said, before either of the others had seen it.

It was true that the sound of its engine was growing fainter, and it faded at about the same time that Peter said, "Gone." His voice was quite positive, though unperturbed.

"That mustn't happen again," said Richard, when he had swallowed the first of his disappointment.

They walked on, and it seemed to Prue that her body had become heavier and her legs more tired than they had been. This is what disappointment does to muscles. But it had started her thinking more clearly, and after a while she stopped and said, "Your lighter, Richard. We could light a fire. Think of the smoke last night's fire made. That'd be even better than plastic."

It seemed, in their gloom, an idea of blinding splendor, and it cheered them immensely. During what was left of the day they listened for the sound of aircraft. The hills gradually drew closer, the brightness gradually withdrew from the air, the sky darkened, and far to the north on the plain the wind began to rise. But, except for a feeling of faint uneasiness, none of them noticed it.

Then, when the sun was already hovering, pinkish, over the outline of the hills, throwing their shadows into long pencil streaks behind them, they heard another aircraft. This time they all heard it simultaneously, and it was Richard who saw it. It was still low on the horizon, but it was coming from the east, toward them. Feverishly they collected dry grass, dead reeds, anything that looked inflammable, piled them with trembling hands on the driest piece of earth they could find, and watched to see the smoke rise as Richard applied his lighter. Four times he managed to strike a spark, and four times a little gust of wind came and blew out the flame. The sound of the plane grew louder, and he squatted down, head low, hands shielding the lighter, and Prue squatted with him, adding the protection of her outspread palms.

"It's coming," said Peter.

Then the little yellow flame licked around a blade of grass, caught, smoked, and a second flame joined the first, together stroking the underside of a second blade of grass, and slowly the fire grew. It was a very frail growth at first, and they tended it with delicate, trembling fingers, but gradually it became more healthy and tiny red coals added to the warmth and little by little a wisp of smoke rose into the air, swelled, and rose higher. Its effect was lessened by the wind, which was now increasing and which swept it along over the plain instead of letting it rise straight and dark into the sky. Now that the fire had really caught, they piled on more grass, watching it grow hot on top and the yellow smoke coil out through it before it burst into flame. More grass yet, and it seemed that anyone looking for three lost people on a plain would see the signal. But even as they waited, full of hope that their time of waiting was ending, Peter said, "It's turning. I think it's going back."

They did not believe him at first, but piled on more grass, blowing it into flames, hurrying it on. But the sound of the engine, which had been getting so loud, now diminished, and Richard and Prue stood up and saw the plane turning in a wide circle, catching the last of the sun so that it shone for a few moments like a silver star and then disappeared into the east, where it had come from, and the sound died away in the quiet evening air. At their feet the fire was burning briskly. They sat down—even Peter—for the disappointment had drained all their energy away.

"I feel sick," said Richard at last.

Prue put her arm around his shoulders. "It'll go," she said. "It isn't anything you ate. Come on. We'll go to the hills."

They walked on toward the hills and toward the deceiving sun, which had shone in the pilot's eyes. It now sat, as red and undazzling as a tomato, on top of the black horizon, leering out under the clouds that began to gather above it. It became half a tomato, a segment of tomato, and then a tiny sliver of vermilion ribbon, and it was gone. Green, pink, yellow, mauve and finally sapphire-blue colored the sky over their heads. The night began, and they went on, pressing to the safety of the hills. Far behind the small fire grew, fanned by the wind, spreading to the nearest tussock, jumping to the next and the next. As the three drew near the first dark slopes the tingling smell of burnt grass came to their nostrils. But they were not accustomed to letting their noses tell them anything. Even Prue and Peter were too much children of the city—of sight and sound. So they took no notice but hurried on.

[5]

I T WAS QUITE DARK when they went in between two outlying shoulders of the hills, up the dry creek bed, under the first overhanging trees. They continued a little way, feeling there was safety in getting deeper into the protecting slopes. Then, finding a level piece of ground surrounded by scrub and shaded by the branches of two ancient white gums, they lay down and went to sleep, too tired to let hunger or thirst keep them awake.

Prue woke from a sleep so deep that she had to float through layers of semiconsciousness before she broke surface—a strange surface—for it was as if she had come through the wrong door, and found herself looking at familiar things from an unfamiliar angle. Peter, she discovered, had been tugging at her hand, and now stood above her, jumping up and down, saying, "Quick, Prue. Wake up! Quick! Hurry!" Still confused, she scrambled to her feet, and for a minute thought that the dizzy feeling,

42

which had been getting better, had returned. But it was not the dizzy feeling; it was the world outside, and this was in a state of terrifying confusion. The wind had risen again and was blowing through the clearing in great gusts, bending the branches of the two big trees above, making them groan, and whipping at the low scrub so that it thrashed all around them as if it were alive. But there was more than this, for a thick fog was blowing through the trees—a thick, blue, hot fog. She choked, coughed, and realized it was not fog at all. It was smoke, and every breath she took was full of the smell of burning eucalyptus.

"Richard!" she screamed.

Richard was already at the edge of the clearing on the side opposite that from which the smoke was coming. He had found a gap in the scrub, and he turned back to shout, "This way. Quick," before he passed through it. Peter now took Prue's hand and pulled her toward it.

"We better go with him, hadn't we? Is he going the right way, Prue? I don't know, do you? But we better go."

Together they ran and plunged through after Richard. They could see him a short distance ahead, scrambling through the bushes, tearing at sarsaparilla tendrils that caught about his legs, tripping, plunging, surging on. And they followed. They did not know which way they were going but only hoped that Richard knew. Sometimes it was up, sometimes down, and sometimes they clambered over rocks, and sometimes found themselves sliding down into gullies from unexpected ridges. Always the smoke followed them, and the wind howled and lashed at the trees. When at last Prue and Peter caught up with Richard, Prue sank down, panting. "I can't go any farther, Richard. I can't go on." Her voice came in a series of gasps.

Richard's clothes were torn and his legs carried a criss-cross of bleeding scratches, but he still stood on his feet, and he shouted back, "You must, Prue. Can't you see the smoke's getting thicker? The fire's traveling faster than we are. We *must* go on." His voice cracked, and he doubled up, coughing.

Peter shouted above the noise, "Then it'll catch us up whether we go on or not. Prue can stop if she wants to."

But Prue got up and they went on. The noise behind them grew louder, and they could hear the crash of falling trees. Bits of flaming twig and leaf began to fall around them. The smoke became thicker and the heat almost unbearable. When they went uphill they now crawled on all fours, and they had long ago given up trying to speak. Their mouths were open and their lips were black with dried spit and smoke and a thin film of ash, encrusted and hard. The flicker of the fire could be seen here and there between the trees, and as they reached the top of a ridge and glanced behind, they saw the soaring, ghost-like trunk of a eucalypt burst into flame—a torch flaring into the sky. Then the roaring, which they had been hearing all the time behind them became louder. Louder and louder, and they saw the flames come leaping through the branches high above, toward them.

Their time had come, and they could only take shelter and cower. Together they tumbled down the far side of the ridge—rolling, sliding, leaping—until they reached the bottom. Here they stayed and crouched in the narrow bed of a dry creek. A few tumbled stones on either side was all the protection they had from the undergrowth that would soon be alight all about them. Richard was on all fours, looking up at the slope down which they had come. Already the trees at the top were blazing, and up the gully toward them, around the point of the ridge, the smoke had begun to roll.

"Dig in!" screamed Peter—a high, piercing small boy's voice. "Prue, dig in." He began to scrabble in the sand and gravel, pressing himself down, making himself small. After one glance at him, Richard did the same. Like animals they were, in among the stones, burrowing out of sight.

But Prue could not burrow. As she tried, with her fingernails or any bits of stick within reach, waves of blackness kept sweeping over her, great gasps, half of nausea, kept shuddering up from the depths of her body. She just recalled being surprised that the gravel felt damp, when she sank full length on her stomach, and another black cloud descended on her as the fire roared up the gully.

She was aware of her back getting hotter and hotter, of the back of her keees prickling and painful, as if stung by wasps, and of her arms automatically going around her head, her hands clutching the back of her neck. Her face was on the gravel, her nose pressed into the sandy bottom, doing its best to breathe for her. Strangely, its tip felt cool and what air she got was cool, too. She pressed her chest, her stomach, her thighs hard into the ground, screwing up her eyes, hanging on to life and breath as best she could. As she lay there she lost the sensation of being a body on the ground; it seemed to her that she was close to some protection, some calm, healing presence with which she had always been deeply familiar but which she had never before known how to approach. As she pressed closer she felt almost as if she were being enfolded, guarded, and whether she was standing or lying she could no longer tell. The pain of her back became remote and unimportant and a great peace wrapped her around. She felt herself submitting to it utterly, and as she lay there, withdrawn to the very center of her living body, she felt the presence move against her, and from within it—or within herself, for she could not tell where it came from—a quiet voice said, "You are safe with me." And she knew that she was and closed her eyes and rested.

A minute—an hour—or a day later she lifted her head and opened her eyes again. There was no pain, and she was no longer hungry or thirsty. Beside her Peter was getting up, and at his feet Richard was sitting with his knees up and his back to a rock. There was a smell of burning and it must come from themselves, for she could see that the clothes on their backs were quite singed and brown. She reached around and rubbed her spine with the back of her hand. Her shirt was in tatters, yet her back was not sore. "I'm not even burnt," she said in surprise.

"Nor me," said Peter. "And is my shirt like yours?" He turned round, presenting her with his bony little shoulder blades.

"Your shirt's burnt," she said. "So's Richard's. Richard, are you all right?"

He was sitting very still, but his eyes, wide and apprehensive, were everywhere. It was a moment before he spoke. "I'm all right—I think," he said. "But where are we?"

Peter ran and squatted down beside him, peering into his face and giving his elbow a little shake. "Here. In the gully. Where we ran from the fire. Remember, Richard? We ran down the hill away from the fire, and this is where it caught us. We dug holes and it went over the top of us. You remember, Richard?" He gave the elbow another impatient shake. Richard was looking at Peter, but his expression was blank and rather helpless.

"It *is* different," said Prue, and sat down beside Richard, close beside him as if for protection.

"It's the same. It's the same," said Peter loudly, and stamped his foot. "You're both silly."

"I wish I were home," said Richard. "In the flat. With Mum. I don't like it."

It was a strange thing for Richard to say—almost an admission of defeat—and after he had said it, they sat for so long that eventually Peter wandered off, saying he would look for the best way out.

Richard looked up at once, alarm in his eyes and in his voice when he spoke. "Where are you going? Don't go far. You might not find the way back."

Peter stopped, grinned, and said, "The way back is what I'm trying to find. Aren't you? Back in a tick." And he skipped off down the gully.

When he had gone, Richard continued to sit motionless and speechless. Prue sat beside him, waiting. Slowly she became aware that on this occasion Richard was not going to lead. She knew that a great uneasiness possessed him and that for the first time he found himself at a loss.

He did not know which way to turn and, not knowing, he could only stay where he was. Glancing sideways at his withdrawn and shuttered face, she wondered how she knew so much of what went on in Richard. But she had no doubt, and now she put her hand lightly on his arm and said, "Richard, what's the matter? What's gone wrong?"

"What's gone wrong?" he said without moving. "That's what I can't make out. Everything's wrong. It's *all* wrong. It feels wrong. Prue, what's happened? What went wrong? Do you think—" He paused, and suddenly his eyes were horrified. "Do you think we could be dead? Do you think we were burnt in the fire?"

Caught off her guard, she laughed and then knew she should not have. Richard really meant it. "No," she said, and slid her arm through his. "We're not dead, Richard. But we might have been. We must have been terribly lucky."

"Why weren't we burnt, then?" he asked slowly. "That's what I can't understand. And if we weren't, what's happened?"

"I don't know."

He said quickly, "But something's happened, hasn't it? Something's wrong somewhere. What is it?"

She could only say, "It's different, but why should it be wrong?"

He turned to her in anger. "Because it's different, that's why. If it's different, of course it's wrong. If you can see it's different then it isn't only me—it can't be only me." Now he clutched tight at his knees with his arms, and once again his eyes roved from side to side.

"No," she said quietly. "It isn't only you." She had

been going to say something reassuring—anything to make him feel at ease. But back into her mind came the memory of the voice that she had heard, the presence she had felt as the fire swept over. It had been obliterated from her mind, but suddenly, like a tide of illumination, it flowed back. The voice was the answer. The voice was the very root of this difference in everything about them, which was still to her so much the same. She opened her mouth to tell him about the voice but looked at his expression and shut it again. She knew she could not tell him and never would be able to. It was the feeling in her that had been induced by the voice that had made everything right. How could one explain a feeling to anyone else? But this was the difference. She had heard the voice and he had not, and she was at peace. She was sure he had not, particularly as she had felt so much involved in its utterance that she had thought it was her own. And because he had not heard it, he was uneasy, even, perhaps, afraid. She could only hold his arm tight and say, "It's not only you, but I'm sure it's nothing to worry about. It's nicer, even. Don't you think it's nicer than we thought?" She looked about her at the great trees, the busy creek, and the calm blue sky.

But Richard only said, "It's different, Prue. And it's wrong. I wish—I almost wish we were still running from the fire."

So THEY SAT, and the strangely tranquil day went on without them, until Richard gave a shiver and said, "Where's Peter? Now where's he got to? He's gone." He got up and was about to charge down the creek when a voice from the slope behind said, "Here I am," and Peter slithered down on the dead leaves until he sat beside them.

"It *is* a bit different," he said. "See, there's no fire."

It was true. There was no sign of a fire in the gully— no wisp of smoke, no smell of burning eucalyptus. There was nothing at all to indicate that so recently a fire had roared through here. Not a smouldering log, not the smallest heap of ashes. In fact the trees that grew about them now were bigger, surely, than those they had seen before the fire came. All around them the ground was damp and carpeted with dead leaves. There was little undergrowth and in their creek—so dry and hard-bottomed when they had last noticed it—a trickle of water was running. The land was the same; the slopes, the gully and the creek; but different trees were growing on it, and no fire had passed this way.

"Why didn't we notice before?" said Prue. "Somehow I never thought about it. I just knew everything was nicer." She turned to Richard and tightened her grasp on his arm. "Richard, that's what it is. You see, the fire must have jumped the creek."

"Look at our shirts," said Richard.

"They could have been singed as we ran," said Prue, rather doubtfully.

50

"You know they weren't." He moved and looked at her. There was no light at all in his eyes. "I can see the fire has never been here, and I can see the creek is running now and it was dry then. That's bad enough, and I noticed that first of all." He shivered and hunched his shoulders. "But that's nothing. There's more. There's something else. We should never have come. We shouldn't be here at all. It's wrong, I keep telling you." He jumped to his feet. "It's as if we'd got into the wrong world. I must get home." The last words were a shout, and for a moment they echoed up the gully.

"Well, come on," said Peter. He pulled at Prue, hopping with impatience. "Come on. We all want to go home. Let's go."

"Where to?" said Prue.

"To a town," said Richard. "To the nearest town as quick as we can."

Prue went to the trickle of water. "I'm going to drink first," she said. "You never know."

They all drank because you never know. But none of them were thirsty. Then they began to follow the creek uphill because Richard said if they got somewhere high they might be able to see a town or a house or a telephone line. And if they only found a telephone line, they could break it and someone would come and fix it.

"How can we break it?" asked Peter. "Can you climb poles?"

Richard could not climb poles, but he had his lighter and he could burn it down. He fished in his pocket. Then he fished in another pocket and finally he said, "I've lost my lighter."

"We won't want it," said Peter promptly. "We won't

find a telephone pole. Come on."

As they walked, they smelled the moist earth warm in the sun. The tall trees were alive with birds, and the ground beneath their feet was dappled with spotted sunshine. All about them was the calmness of well-being and of peace. It must have been morning, for the sun, which had been shining through the tree trunks, was high above the branches now. There was no sign of yesterday's—if it was yesterday's—terror and turmoil. Yesterday might never have been. The benign calm affected them all, and little by little their spirits rose. No longer plagued by hunger, no longer tired, they began to enjoy the morning, forgetting yesterday and tomorrow.

The gully they followed began to grow smaller, and they came to the source of the little creek—a rocky basin shaded and lined with maidenhair out of which the water bubbled up. From here it was not far to the top. The ground flattened, out and a little breeze, fresh and untainted, blew in their faces and cooled them. Ahead the country stretched away, flat and far, and the trees grew tall and straight. Long strands of bark hung from many of them, swaying in the lightly moving air and making a hushing sound against the shining trunks. Farther off they could see patches of sunlight on grassy glades and clumps of trees that were smaller and greener than the eucalypts, which might have been wattles or acacias. They turned and looked behind them, and now it was possible to see clear over the lower treetops to the plains beyond. Prue felt a momentary sense of relief that the plains were there at all.

There was no sign of the fire on the plains, either. They stretched eastward as they had last seen them, a rolling, browny-green and in the distance the cattle had reappeared. But the grass was longer than they remembered, for every so often it was bent over in the passing breeze, rippling like a gray-green sea. And as they looked more closely, the cattle seemed to have changed their shape. They were far away, but even so, there was something unfamiliar about their grouping and the way they moved. Or was it only their shape?

"I don't believe they are cattle," said Prue. "I think they're emus."

Peter said he was sure they were walking on two long legs each, like bundles of feathers on sticks, but Richard said he could not possibly see so much at such a distance. In his view it was cattle, and if they thought otherwise, then something funny had happened to their eyesight. Plenty of funny things were happening, anyway, he said bitterly, and this would not be very strange. But he had to admit that there was no sign of a house or any other activity of man. And so they turned their backs on the plain and went on through the trees.

About an hour later, although they had ceased to measure time by hours, Richard said, "I could swear it was the springtime, but we left Sydney in late summer. Remember how hot it was?"

"Perhaps we're just high up," said Prue.

"But we're not. We were going downstream all the time out of that first gorge. Then it was flat, and it's only today we've been going up."

"Well, it is spring," said Peter. "Who cares? I don't. I like it." He shuffled happily through the dead leaves, making two trails, like a railway line, behind him.

"It can't be," said Richard. "Don't be so stupid."

"He's only little, Richard," said Prue quickly.

"I'm not," shouted Peter. "I'm big. I'm bigger than you," and he jumped up and caught the lowest branch of the nearest tree, swinging himself up until he looked down on both of them. "And it's spring. It's spring. It's spring!" He jumped down and ran on ahead.

"Kids never care," said Richard.

Prue walked beside him, but she felt like running, too. For the first time since the accident her head felt quite clear. It did not ache any more. She felt well, and she could not care, either.

All day, as the sun traveled across the sky, they walked through the trees. Threading their way through the colonnades of trunks, they felt as tiny as ants. Once Prue stopped, sniffed, and said, "I smell wattle. It must be spring," and then came upon the blaze of yellow in a clearing.

"I read that all the year round there's some species of wattle in flower," said Richard.

Toward late afternoon when the sun again streamed through the tree trunks, the ground began to open out. Shrubs and a thin covering of undergrowth spread over the more open ground, and sometimes patches of grass indicated a change in the type of country. They had been walking in silence for some time, and the only sounds about them had been small sounds—the buzzing of flies, the chirp of some small bird—when, some distance away they heard the sound of something large moving through the undergrowth. Caution and a sense that the surrounding bush was strangely unfamiliar made them run to the nearest group of trees. But they need not have bothered. As they watched, peering from behind the protecting trunks, they saw the tops of some shrubs begin to wave. Then a large mob of red kangaroos bounded into the clearing. With something like relief they stepped out from among the trees to watch. At first they were not seen, and the kangaroos came bounding forward, front paws tucked neatly into chests, springing tails waving up and down. There must have been twenty or thirty, and they were all sizes. A tremendous old-man kangaroo led them and close on his heels bounded does, young males, and here and there a joey that had only recently outgrown his mother's pouch. They were moving quite calmly but in a set direction. The old man saw the children first and came to a sudden halt. They all stopped, and there was complete silence as they froze, heads up, ears pricked, and soft brown eyes all turned in the same direction. The last of the sunlight, pink now, streamed through the clearing. Somewhere in the branches above a bird shrieked. Then the old man made a sound between a snort and a sneeze, turned and bounded off into the trees. His mob followed, and soon the crashing of their departure died away.

"Oh," said Prue, and smiled.

"They weren't scared, really," said Peter. "It's their home here. Not ours." It was a funny thing to say, but at seven one must be expected to say some funny things.

Only Richard said nothing but stared after them. Presently he gave a shiver and turned away.

The day was growing old, and they went on, for it would soon be time to find somewhere to sleep. Now the ground once again became more uneven. Among the low, scrubby hills were rocky outcrops of granite. A species of low, spreading tea tree grew in the hollows, taking advantage of the dampness, and the white, twisted limbs looked ghostly in the half light. They were about to decide on the shelter of one of these tea-tree clumps when the night breeze, wafting from over the rising ground to the west, brought a smell that halted them at once. They stood like pointers, noses to the breeze. No one spoke. No one breathed, except to savor, delicately, tentatively, unbelievingly, the message brought to them on the soft eddies of the evening air. Silently they turned to one another, eyes wide, mouths half open. Richard spoke first.

"I smell smoke. And someone's cooking meat."

Prue had a fancy that he expected them to say that they could not smell it. But she smelled it too, and Peter simply said, "Come on. Quick."

[7]

THEY SET OFF TOGETHER, running fast, for the rise on the far side of the hollow. Only people cooked their food. Only people light a fire at dusk and make themselves a meal. It was the thought of people even more than the thought of food that spurred them on. Richard bounded ahead, too eager to greet again the things he knew to wait for the others.

But they caught him up again at the top of the rise. He was standing with his legs apart, hands on hips, a frown on his forehead, gazing at the countryside that fell away in long, gentle slopes on the far side of the rise. It was becoming hard to see, for blue shadows were flowing up from the low-lying areas, and above the air was filled with the dazzle of the last sunlight. As during so much of this day, there was a great stillness everywhere, seeming intensified now as the land waited for the night. Somewhere below and far away a crow cawed—a desolate, echoing sound. Directly below, the slope was clear and turfed with coarse grass, but farther down the bush began and rolled away thick and dark to the west. There was no sign at all of human habitation.

"Where is the smoke coming from?" said Richard. "I thought we'd see a town." His voice was flat with disappointment.

Hearing it, Prue felt a sudden stab of pity. But she wondered why the idea of a town had not come to her at all. "There might not be a town," she said gently, "but someone's cooking his dinner down there." And she smiled into his harassed face.

They could still smell the smoke—pungent and full of the odors of roasting meat. In the gathering gloom it was now almost impossible to see anything in the bush below, and it was clear that no fire burned on the grassy slope before them. It was a fine, cool evening, full of the surge of spring—of the smell of earth and drying grass and some aromatic herb crushed by their feet. And there was a mellow softness hinting at the heat of summer to come. Everywhere there was a peace so deep that it almost silenced the beating of their hearts. Prue felt it and knew that she was being taken care of; Peter felt it and unthinkingly accepted it as his birthright. But Richard kicked at a stone with his foot and shouted, "Where are they? Where's the fire? How shall we find them in the dark?" His head was constantly turning as he searched the sea of treetops far below.

Prue took him by the wrist and pulled him to the

ground. "Sit down, Richard," she said. "Sit down and wait—and watch. When it's dark enough we'll see the light of the fire."

"I never thought of that," he said, as he sat down. "I never thought of it. Of course. We'll easily see the light of the fire."

They waited, sitting on the hillside, and the tides of night rolled up from the low-lying parts, blotting out the trees and the slopes below. In a tussock not far away the first cricket turned himself on, and as the western sky faded, the stars pricked out in the luminous blue overhead.

"Did someone speak?" said Richard.

"We must be careful," said Prue, and did not know why she said it.

"I been looking," said Peter. "An' I can see it."

"What?" said Prue, and suddenly felt frightened of the answer.

"The fire, silly. What we've been looking for."

"Where?" said Richard loudly, and jumped up. "Peter, where? I can't see it."

"Yes, you can. Look where I point."

Richard had to squat down to look along the line of the bony arm to where one dirt-encrusted finger hovered over the western landscape. At last he sighed, and it was a sound of deep relief. He got up. "Yes," he said. "That's it. Come on. Let's go."

He had started off down the slope when Prue said, "Richard. Wait."

He halted and turned. "Why? Come on, Prue. We don't want to lose it."

She could not explain the sudden feeling of apprehension, the sure, but unexplainable knowledge that this unknown could be dangerous. "It might be men," was all she could think of to say.

Richard gave a great laugh. "Well, naturally. That's what we're expecting, isn't it? Come on, Prue, for goodness' sake. It's men we're looking for."

"Peter!" She had not meant it to be a call for help. But the tone she used turned it into one. It surprised her as much as it surprised Richard, who was accustomed to having his views accepted by Prue without question.

Peter was on all fours, sniffing and looking. At Prue's voice he squatted back on his haunches. "That's it all right. Smell's coming from there." He got up. "We got to go, Prue. It's meant for us, you know. But we'll be careful. Come on." He plunged off down the hill.

"What's he talking about?" said Richard.

"I don't know," said Prue. But she had a feeling that she ought to. Somehow, what he had said was what she wanted to hear. Her confidence returned, and she stepped off down the hill, following Richard as she always did.

With the thickening of night the fire became more and more easy to see, and while they had it in sight, they ran on down the hill. At last they had come down so far that the beginnings of the bush loomed darkly ahead, and because of the treetops they could no longer see the fire. They stopped and drew together. Now it was Richard's turn.

"We'll stay together," he said. "We'll have to remember where we last saw the fire, and we'll have the smell to help us." He was eager and his eyes were bright. The ring had come back into his voice. "Stay close to me." He

59

walked toward the trees, and the twigs and dried leaves cracked and crunched beneath his feet.

"Not so loud," said Peter. "They don't like noises in the night."

"What's he talking about?" said Richard for the second time. But he began to walk more carefully.

Soon they left the grass behind, made their way through the fringe of scrub, and slipped in among the trees. They became engulfed in darkness, and the trees towered overhead, whispering, rustling, and breathing all about them.

"Can you smell the smoke?" said Richard. "Where's it coming from?"

"Shssh!" said Prue. "We mustn't make a noise."

"Why not?" said Richard loudly. "What's come over you two? You and Peter—you both want us to creep about. What's the matter with you both? We're going to find these people. Remember? They'll look after us now. There's nothing to worry about so long as we find them."

"I just think," said Peter, "it's better to creep till we know what sort of men they are."

"You're scared," said Richard. But he recalled that Peter was only seven and added, "You don't have to be. You keep close to me. You'll be all right." He felt a tug at his shirt, and Prue's voice in his ear, "Please, please be quiet, Richard. I'm sure we must."

It was her tone rather than the words that gave him his first twinge of uneasiness—just enough to make him say, "Very well, if you're both scared. Just so long as we find them." And they went on again silently through the trees, stepping warily among the dry sticks and rustling bark and stopping now and then to sniff.

After a short time they could not have returned to the open slopes if they had wanted to. They were engulfed in the forest. It was living its own ruthless, sightless life, and they had no part in it. Overhead millions of invisible leaves were busy with the light wind and below, where they walked, small things chirruped, creaked, whispered, and scuttled. And under their feet the great roots spread out, burrowing in the secret earth, gathering food and drink for the trees they nourished. There was no need to tell Richard to be quiet now. Even he had begun to feel an unwanted stranger, and even he walked softly and took care he did not brush too hard against a sapling or a low-hanging branch. He drew nearer to the still invisible fire with the beginnings of apprehension.

They seemed to have walked for miles when Prue and Richard simultaneously felt their elbows grasped, and Peter, with his wiry fingers pressed hard to the bone, made them stop. His face was only a pale blur in the darkness, but they bent to hear him whisper. "Look. Look there."

Neither of them could see anything but blackness, but then Prue fancied she could see the dim shape of a tree trunk far ahead. She rubbed her eyes and blinked, for the tree trunk glowed faintly pink and seemed to be moving. She stared at it and found she was seeing not one but three or four tree trunks and above them, faintly outlined, the shapes of branches. But it seemed to her that they were dancing, for they swayed and leaped together. Then, suddenly, she understood. It was the fire, still invisible, but shining up into the trees, and the flickering flames were dancing and not the trees. She heard Richard let out a long, quivering breath and knew that he had seen it too. She wondered if he would shout and charge ahead. But he did not.

"Stay close to me," he whispered, and they went furtively toward the glowing tree trunks.

The smell of the smoke and roasting meat was very strong now, and after a time they began to see the smoke curling among the branches. More trees became visible until they formed a circle, and the branches overhanging the fire could be clearly seen. But still they could not see the fire itself or who was sitting beside it, cooking his dinner. As they drew nearer Prue began to wonder if it was nothing more than a dream, for there was something unreal about the night. She knew that Richard and Peter could feel it too, for they were too tense and silent. Then, above the forest noises, to which they were becoming accustomed, the wind carried them the first sounds of crackling, burning twigs. Immediately they slackened their pace and, still grasping each other tightly, began to take cover behind the tree trunks. For a few minutes they slipped silently from trunk to trunk, pausing behind each to·look and listen. And during one such pause they heard quite clearly the sound of human voices. These were the first human sounds except their own that any of them had heard since the accident, and at first Prue thought she must have forgotten what a group of people talking sounded like. Then she knew that she had not forgotten. These sounds were of a kind that she had never heard before. They were sharp, high, and nasal and seemed to be ejaculated in short bursts, more like the sounds of animals than people.

For a long time they remained behind the tree, waiting and listening. Not even Richard could make the decision to go forward. Yet none of them knew why they hesitated. People were what they had set out to find, and here were people. Yet—they could not move. It was as if a spell held them. The fire crackled, the ragged, guttural sounds went on, and the forest around them pursued its normal nocturnal course. Above their heads the branches waved and whispered. Not far away an owl hooted. Each of them jerked as if an electric shock had passed through the tree they pressed against. Their ears and eyes were strained; their bodies utterly still.

At last, into Prue's listening ears a voice came. She clearly understood the words. "Go forward quietly. Be gentle but unafraid." The sound was like nothing she had ever heard, yet it was like every sound she had ever heard. It rang like a bell among the trees, it came up like thunder from the ground, it whispered in the rustling wind, and it echoed through the forest like a great gong. After a time its reverberations died away, and she let out a long-held breath. She took Richard and Peter by the hand.

"Come along," she said softly.

To her surprise Peter whispered back, "Not scared, but slow. I'm coming." But Richard only murmured in her ear, "I didn't like that sudden gust of wind."

They went forward, still from tree to tree, until they were able to see the fire itself. And when they could see that, they could see also who tended it and who sat beside it. They could not have said what they had expected to see, but it surprised them all to find that it was a group of Aborigines. So far they had not been seen. The Aborigines were grouped around the fire in an open space among the trees. There must have been twenty people gathered there. A great many were tall men with long, thin, chocolate-colored legs and arms and the aboriginal faces the children recognized—full lips, strong jaws, flat noses and low foreheads. Many of them wore beards, and all had tousled heads of black, wavy hair. There were many women, too, of all ages, and some were playing with small children. The fire, which seemed to be made on a big mound of ashes, was dying down now, but several of the women were busy poking about with sticks among the ashes below the glowing logs. To the right of the clearing there was a collection of low shelters made of bent slabs of bark. They were not more than four feet high and could only be entered by crawling. One thin, yellow dog poked about among them and then lay down with its head to the fire. And now and then it licked its lips and began to pant. No one took any notice of it.

They stood silently and watched for what seemed a very long time. And as they watched, Prue noticed two things. One was that, contrary to any Aborigines she had ever seen, these wore no clothes at all. Except for a few of the men, who wore thin pieces of twine about their waists, from which dangled in front bunches of leaves, none wore any kind of garment. There was not a piece of cloth among the lot of them. The second thing was that there was not a metal object anywhere to be seen either. Even near the fire where their meal was being prepared, there was not one pot or pan. It was as if they had never seen a white man—never been near a town or a railhead.

But the voice that Prue had heard still drove her forward, and with Peter walking beside her, she stepped into the clearing. Richard, who had hesitated on the edge of the firelight, now saw that he was being left behind, and he ran after them. He had not wished to enter the clearing, but he was the protector, and if the other two went, he must be there to guard them. Prue and Peter had not been noticed by the Aborigines, but Richard's hurried approach was far from silent, and it caused the whole group to jump to its feet, swinging around to face them. In a moment the men had gathered in front of the women and children, and some, as they jumped, had snatched up spears or clubs. The dog began to bark and bounded toward them. But when it was some six yards from them, it stopped dead, digging its claws into the ground and slithering on stiff forelegs. Though thin, it was a large dog with savage teeth, and its hackles were standing stiff along the spine. It stood barking, and saliva began to trickle from its mouth.

Some of the men had begun to shout, but now as they stood hesitating, watching the three children, they became silent. Prue and Peter stood facing the group, their hands by their sides. Richard, beside them, was motionless too, but his eyes were everywhere and only a frustrated feeling of not knowing what to do next held him still. The Aborigines continued to gaze at them, and they continued to wait until Prue, who stood beside Richard, felt him prepare to move. She spoke softly, without turning her head. "What are you doing, Richard?"

"Come back," he said between his teeth. "It's not safe here. Come back." And he made a movement to pull her back among the trees. At this the men started forward and some made sharp, angry noises. One drew back his spear and took aim.

Then, in the middle of the tension, a child broke loose. A naked brown toddler, shining with grease, pushed through the tightening ranks of men and ran toward Peter. It kicked at the dog, laughing, and still laughing ran to Peter with its hands out. The dog stopped barking, quickly licked its jaws, transferred its gaze to the child, and began to pant again. A buzz of angry sound rose from the clustered men, but now the child was in the way of their spears, and they hesitated.

It seemed as if Peter did not notice the display of hostile strength facing him, for he laughed back at the child, knelt down and put out his hands. The child flung himself forward, and they both fell over. Now Prue bent down, put out her hands and holding one hand of each, pulled them both to their feet. The men had fallen silent. She walked forward, leading them toward the waiting men. The baby trotted and gurgled on one side and Peter pranced, unconcerned, on the other. He looked up at Prue.

"He's a great little kid, isn't he? But he smells."

The line of men was quite silent as Prue went up to them. When she was about nine feet from them, the nearest took a step back. She stopped and the baby promptly sat down in the dust. Gentle but unafraid. The words were still in her mind. She lifted her head and looked them in the face, smiled, and bent down to pick up the baby. Then she held it out to the nearest man. It was heavy and she staggered. When he did not immediately step forward, a sudden burble of words rose up from among them. The others gathered around, and some tried to push him forward. He resisted, leaning back, making sounds of excited protest, and his eyes began to roll. Prue laughed and put the baby down. Then Peter took it by the hand and took a few steps forward.

Straight away the men fell back. But now there was a movement and a shuffling behind them. They surged about for a few moments, and then a woman pushed her way through, elbowing out of her way the man that had refused to go forward, and strode up to the baby. She bent down, jabbering to the men as she did so, swept it up, and was about to retreat when she stopped, looked at Peter carefully and, putting a brown hand about his neck, drew him forward with her into the crowd.

"Hey! Hold it!"

It was Richard, shouting from behind her. Prue turned quickly, clutched him as he was about to run forward, and put herself between him and the suddenly raised spears. "Don't do anything. Wait." Then, when she felt him stop trying to push her out of the way, "I think it will be all right. Just wait."

He looked at her incredulously. "How can you be so sure? We could easily not see him again."

"You can't help him. But he'll be all right. She will look after him."

"She? Who? That woman?" Richard sounded as if he thought her mad. Speechlessly, she shook her head. She had not meant the aboriginal woman. She did not know whom she meant. The words had just slipped out. She could not think why she had said them. But Richard stopped, and the spears were lowered.

"We had better just wait," she said at last. "I think they are afraid of us. I don't know why."

So they waited, standing together facing the flickering firelight so that their faces glowed pink. The dog turned and slunk back to the shelters, eyeing them as it went, its hackles not quite lowered. The men, also eyeing them, began to move about. Some turned to the fire, some sat down, but some—those that held the spears—still stood quiet but watchful. There was no sign of Peter, but some women were busy at the fire, and the smell of meat suddenly came to them, strong and appetizing. Prue swallowed. She had not felt hungry, but she remembered it was a long time since she had eaten. There was a sudden babble of sound, several of the women were moving about, and now one came toward them. She was being pulled by Peter, who was carrying on a conversation, totally unintelligible to her, telling her not to be frightened, introducing her to Prue and Richard, telling her about the fire, using his very best social manner as he half led, half pushed her toward them. She was carrying something in her hands, and at first she had been apprehensive, eyes wide and little squeaks of protest coming from her mouth. But as Peter talked she began to relax. Then she smiled. Then she began to giggle, and her white teeth flashed. Then, nodding and giggling as Peter continued to talk, she came without fear toward them. She held out her hands, and they saw that they held something warm and dripping, and the smell was tantalizing.

"Go on," said Peter. "Take it. It's food. She's giving it to you."

So they took it and sat down where they were and ate. They did not know what they were eating, for it was black and unrecognizable. Red juice ran out when they bit into it. But they did not care. They could feel the warmth and strength seeping back into their bodies. Seeing how hungry they were, the Aborigines brought them more and, losing their fear as Richard was losing his, began to gather around them, laughing and talking and wondering with their faces and their hands, as they reached out from time to time and touched the white skin. After his fourth piece of meat, Peter stretched, belched, and yawned. His face glistened greasily in the firelight. "I'm sleepy," he said. "I don't think I can keep awake much longer." He got up and walked toward the fire, a small, tattered, thin-legged, scabby-kneed boy, but unafraid and living in a world of simple wants and problems.

Near the fire a tumbled heap of brown children and babies had settled down for the night. Peter went up to them, looked about pensively, hands on hips for a moment, and then lay down, wriggled, put his head on a small brown thigh, and shut his eyes. He sighed heavily, twitched once, and they saw his hands relax in sleep.

"Now what?" said Richard. "What do we do now? Stand guard over him? I'm tired."

Looking at his drooping shoulders and his sunken, half-closed eyes, Prue knew that it was true. He was deathly tired. If they attacked him now, he could do no more. She and Peter had come unscathed through the past hour. But Richard had fought with the tremendous tensions of uncertainty and fear. His resilience was at an end. "We can sleep too," she said. "It will be all right. We can sleep here."

But when they lay down, stretching themselves on the leafy ground, the men started to chatter among themselves. One came up to them, touched Prue on the shoulder as if her white skin might have been red hot, and pointed to one of the bark shelters on the edge of the clearing. Somehow she persuaded Richard to get up, and she helped him stagger toward it. There comes a time when one is too tired for fear, and Richard was now past emotion of any kind. He was asleep as he crawled on all fours into the tent. Prue lay down beside him, feeling more strongly than she had felt before that she was enveloped in a different air—a protective atmosphere—that kept her apart and untouched. She had felt like this in dreams, but this was not a dream. Before she fell asleep, she was disturbed by a shuffling at her feet and saw that the sleeping body of Peter had been carried to the opening and pushed into the hut beside her. He gave one sleepy groan, wriggled once, and settled down like a warm puppy in the small of her back.

[8]

I T WAS THE VOICE that woke Prue. It was ringing in her head and echoing all about her. "Run! Run!" it was saying. All around her was noise and turbulence. Somewhere there was danger, but she could not tell where. Her head had begun to ache again.

"Run! Run!"

But her legs would not work. Her feet were too heavy to lift. She gasped and opened her eyes. As she opened them memory came surging back. She was in the shelter and there were Aborigines and a warm fire. She closed her eyes again, opened them a second time, and blinked. A tremor ran through her body, and she felt her stomach twitch and contract. There was no shelter. There was nothing but mist—swirling, gray, damp mist. And in the mist was a great noise, and the voice, saying, "Run!

Run!" She put out her hands and felt about her desperately. Stretching at arm's length, she felt the warmth of Richard's body, and the relief brought tears to her eyes. The feeling of desolation, of being the only living thing, had been familiar and horrible. He stirred as she thumped his thigh. When she tried to get up, she felt her leg held. It was the dream returned, and for a moment she felt icy cold. But an ordinary voice was saying, "Quick, Prue! Get up. We got to run." It was Peter's voice, and he was trying to pull her out of the no-longer-existing bark shelter.

"Let go," she shouted in the tumult. "I'm coming." She felt her leg released and struggled to her feet. She sensed Richard scrambling up beside her. He began to shout, "What's happened? Where are we? I can't see anything in this damned fog. Prue!"

She reached for his hand, the words, "Run! Run!" still ringing in the swirling mists. She felt Peter's fingers clutch her other wrist and pull.

"Come on. Quick!" he shouted.

She found that they were standing on a steep slope. "Where?" she shouted. "Which way?"

"This way," shouted Peter, and began to pull her downhill. Dragging Richard with her, she started to run, and Peter's fingers clutched harder and pulled her faster and faster. The ground was hard and jagged underfoot, and at times slippery like glass. They struggled to keep their feet, because to fall would drag them all to some half-guessed-at abyss. All around them the crashing, booming and shrieking went on, and they tried to close their ears and think of nothing but escape. When they had gone a little way, the mist began to thin. They could see great clouds of it, wreathing about them, and sometimes a gap that showed them more distant swirling clouds. At the same time they began to get cold. They were panting with exertion and should have been hot, but from the middle of their bones a killing, numbing cold began to creep. They could feel it spread along their limbs to their fingers and toes, and the air that they drew in through their nostrils felt as if it were setting solid in their lungs.

"Faster!" shouted Peter.

Somehow they produced the energy for extra speed. Somehow they fought off the crippling cold, and at last going downward through the mist, they felt a warmer air. It began to react on the mist, which was much thinner now, and as they ran, they peered through it, trying to find out where they were. There was a sudden belch of very warm air from somewhere below them, the last of the mist swirled away, and all three of them came to a dead stop. They clung together, staring.

Above them the mists still boiled and rolled, but to their left, down a tremendous fall of land a great glacier spread out like a glittering ribbon of white. It widened as it descended, but they could not see where it ended, for the ridge on which they stood loomed up in between. They saw now what they had been running on. They saw why it had felt so sharp and rough. It was nothing but black rock that glittered here and there and that looked as if it had been boiling and then frozen. Not one blade of grass grew on it, not one speck of lichen. It was utterly bare, black, and dead. The head of the glacier was lost in the mist, but beyond it, farther to their left, they could see the skyline. It was a skyline such as they had never seen.

72

For the whole visible length it was spiked with black mountain peaks. And the mountains themselves fell away into gorges and ridges as black as the one they stood on. Here and there a gorge had changed from black to white, and they guessed it was the beginning of a more distant glacier. The sky above the mountain peaks glowed greeny-yellow with here and there a fleck of red. A thin pencil line of gray mist hung horizontally over the peaks, backed by the yellow light of the sky. But when they looked more carefully, they saw it was not mist.

Richard said in an appalled whisper, "It's not mist. It's smoke. Those aren't ordinary mountains. Those are volcanoes. And they're active. Nearly all of them are smoking." Nobody answered him, but behind them in the mist a great rumble and a hiss seemed to give a reply. Suddenly Richard shouted, "Where are we? In heaven's name, where are we?" His voice echoed among the dead, black rocks, and an answering roar came out of the mist. This time there were words in the roar. They were, "Run! Run!"

"What was that?" shouted Richard. "What was that? Did you hear?"

Prue said, "It's the voice again, and we must run." Her own voice trembled as she spoke.

Richard looked at her distractedly. "What voice? What are you talking about? Whose voice? Prue, are you all right?" And he took her shoulder roughly and shook it.

When he had let her go, she said, "Didn't you hear it? Don't you ever hear it?"

He looked at her in a trembling silence and then said, "Prue, does your head still ache?" She nodded and knew that it was some kind of betrayal. Her head was aching, but it was not the right answer.

"Well, come on, then," Peter was shouting. "We won't get out if we don't." He pulled them both forward down the cruel black slope, and they had no time to protest.

They left the mists behind, and the air became warmer every minute. But they stopped for breath once, and while they were motionless, they felt a quivering beneath their feet. They looked at one another with whitening faces, and the quivering increased until it shook them where they stood, and they nearly fell over. With it came a kind of rumble from below. And the rock they stood on seemed, like an escalator, to move slowly forward. Here and there came tiny cracks from which oozed a steaming, viscous liquid, as if the rock were bleeding. But the liquid was a shining black.

"It's not rock at all," shouted Richard. "It's lava! And it's molten underneath. That's why it's moving. It's only a crust we're standing on."

A sudden panic fear possessed them, and they ran on, knowing there was danger and it was everywhere. They made for the farthest, lowest point of the ridge, for there was nowhere else to run. They dared not look behind, but they could not block their ears, and behind them the rumbling grew louder. They slipped and stumbled, and sometimes they knew it was because the lava moved beneath them. They did not know what they were running toward but remembered only the unknown danger behind them.

At last they reached the point of the ridge and stopped short, because the rock fell away almost sheer to meet the glacier that swept in a great curve about its foot. They could see now what lay at the foot of the right-hand slope of the ridge. Below them for miles stretched a great, dark lake. Here, near the point of the ridge, it lapped far below up to the very foot of the slope and farther off where the glacier entered it, great lumps of ice broke off and floated away in the distance, like swans on the black water. The far shore of the lake was lost in mists. But beyond it, very faint on the white skyline, was another mountain range. It was too far away to tell if the peaks were volcanoes, but they were sharp as needles.

Where the lake curved away from the ridge, leaving a widening strip of level ground in between, there was some kind of forest growing, or it may have been low scrub, for they looked down on the tops of the tossing, feathery branches. The over-all color of the trees or shrubs was a deep, rich green.

Prue saw it with a feeling of tremendous relief. At first she scarcely understood why this should be, but later knew it was because the trees were living. In this vast, terrifying landscape of utter non-life, the trees alone pursued a comforting organic existence. Somehow, too, they held out a hope of rescue. She knew that if they could reach the trees they would be safe. The other two must have felt the same, for Richard said as soon as he could catch his breath, "But how do we get down? We'll have to find a way."

Peter was leaning far out over the slope, edging away from the top of the ridge, but he said over his shoulder, "There's no path. And it's steep as a house."

Now that they stood still they could feel again the movement underfoot. It seemed impossible that such a hard surface could move at all, but when the quivering was at its height, they could see the surface heave and roll. The rumbling was almost deafening now.

Prue found her arm grabbed and Peter at her side, and he was pointing to the left, where the glacier wound its way up to the distant peaks. "What's that?" he shouted in her ear. "See? Out there. Out there."

At first she could not see anything, but she put her arm around his shoulders and held him tight. They all stared at the gleaming white expanse of the glacier. Then Richard made a sudden sharp sound. The face of the glacier was moving. Some way back from the point of the ridge the ice was heaving, swelling, and then subsiding, as if some gigantic force beneath were struggling for release. All along its length as far as they could see, the ice began to move, and where it met the lake, the water rippled and splashed.

Out in the middle of the glacier the ice rose higher and they were suddenly deafened by a series of tremendous shrieks and crashes. The glacier was cracking, and where it cracked, wisps of steam now rose up into the air. The bulge grew bigger, the shrieks turned to ear-splitting explosions, and more steam poured out through the widening cracks.

They staggered as the lava crust moved wildly, too paralyzed with fear to run, for they had nowhere to run, and there was no one to care whether they ran or not. In this cataclysmic drama they had no place, and there was no pity in the ground they stood on. Peter shouted something to Richard, but they only saw his lips move. Then there came a tremendous explosion, the ridge shook, and the ice in the middle of the bulge split open, upended in great white slabs like cliffs, rearing up and sliding back endways, so that they remained like gigantic heaps of

76

broken glass. Smoke, flames, and belching vapor burst out and rose into the sky, scattering red hot rocks which bounced and thudded as they fell back on to the ice, and a great cloud of steam rose from the entire surface of the glacier and spread out like a blanket of fog, obliterating everything and rolling at speed down the slope of the glacier toward the ridge where they stood. The explosions continued and the pain in their ears was agonizing. They had been flung to the ground, and they scrambled to their feet, only to be flung down again. The mist rolled closer. They could smell the sulphurous vapor now, and they all knew that it was not mist but steam and could burn them where they stood.

"Help! Oh, help!" screamed Prue, and the mist billowed up the side of the ridge and enveloped them. She waved her arms and gasped, wide-eyed, and as she fought with this impossible enemy it seemed to her that the clouds of mist before her rolled together, glowing with a pearly light, and formed a kind of shape. It became a tall figure—an immensely tall figure—and the robe that fell from the shoulders to the feet was mist, and the head, wild-haired, shone as if the essence of all sunlight were settled there, and the eyes glowed huge and bright, and it seemed to Prue that they were fixed on her. The shoulders, like distant mountain ridges, bent toward her, the face bowed fleetingly over her head, and at once she felt a quietness all about her, and from the bowed head came a gentle warmth that calmed the tattered nerve ends and filled her with fresh strength. She shut her eyes and thought the palm of a hand was placed on her hair. Her heart stopped its frantic fluttering, the panic fear left her, and she opened her eyes. There was no figure there, but the mist was all about them, moist, sulphurous, and hot, and growing hotter with every new flush of steam up the side of the ridge. Richard and Peter were on their stomachs on the lava surface, their arms about their heads. She bent down, tugging at their sleeves, until they raised their heads.

"Come on," she shouted, and they read the words in the movement of her lips. She ran toward the edge of the ridge, to the side where, far below, the green branches offered shelter. With perfect confidence she stepped out onto the frightening slope, somehow kept her feet, and began to go down. Behind her the two boys followed.

They never knew how they got to the bottom without falling. Several times one or other of them stumbled. Once Peter went down on both knees, and only Richard, blocking him from below, prevented him rolling to the bottom. They should have been cut and scratched. They should have been bleeding and bruised from countless contacts with the sharp edges of the lava. But they were not. There was no mark on any of them. At their backs the ridge rose, black and forbidding, and there was no sign of the path, if path there had been, that they had used to come down. Along the top of the ridge the mist hung and billowed but came no farther. The inferno of noise still went on, but down here it was muffled, and they were able to speak again.

Prue touched each boy in turn. "Are you all right?" she asked. They nodded, for now that they might speak there were no words to fit their thoughts.

They looked about them. To their left along the foot of the ridge lay the lake. Waves were breaking and splashing now against the rocks, for the glacier's movement had agitated the whole surface of the water as far as they could see. Ahead of them, across a flat swamp where tufted grasses grew, the forest began. They could see now that it was a true forest, for the trees grew thick and high. From here their shape looked strange, but they offered protection and a kind of hope, and so they set off across the squelchy tussocks toward it. The air here was warm and heavy, smelling still of sulphur, but with a damp decay added that clung about their nostrils. The ground they trod on was black and rather sandy, and on the drier patches a kind of moss was growing.

Before long they reached the edge of the forest. It was the strangest forest they had ever seen. The tall trees that made up the greater part of it had long, rough trunks to which a few dead branches were still attached that swung, rustling, in the wind. But the bulk of the branches all grew from a point at the top of the trunk, spreading out rather like an umbrella. The branches themselves were like great fern fronds and lifted and fell with the wind. Among them grew long, tubular plants, looking more like giant asparagus than anything else. They grew here and there among the big trees to a height of eight feet or more, and at regular intervals around their stems grew little rows of tiny leaves. These seemed to like the damper places and grew wherever there were puddles. There were also numbers of pretty little ferns along the floor of the forest, and here and there where the sun penetrated grew large clumps of wire-like grasses. They walked in among the trunks, and the forest closed over them.

ALL THE REST OF THAT DAY they walked, and although they had no idea where they might be going, their thought was only of escape, and they walked till they could walk no more. The light was fading, and the forest was beginning to look very vast and black and endless when they stopped for the night. They found a dry place on the flat ground and sank down at the foot of one of the big trees. High above, the fernlike branches rose and fell and covered them like a green roof. They looked about for insects that might bite or sting but found none.

"Not even an ant," said Peter, scrabbling in the earth beside him.

"Thank goodness for that," said Richard. "We've had enough for one day." He paused before he went on. "I can't talk about it. I can't *think* about it. Can you, Prue?"

Prue said quietly, "No. I don't seem to be able to think at all. I don't know where we are, and I don't know why we're here. But, Richard, I think we'll find our way out." She knew it was true, but she hoped he would not ask her how she knew. She had only said it because she wanted to make him feel better.

They lay down close together, and for a time they all stared at the green roof above. With the end of day the wind was dropping and the forest became very still. They could no longer hear the terrible noise of the eruption and the breaking glacier, but faintly in the distance it was possible to hear the lake, for the waves were crashing everywhere along the shore. Apart from this, there was no sound at all. They slept all night, for there was nothing to disturb them.

Peter woke first to find the sun streaming through the tree trunks along the forest floor. He lay and watched it for a time, then he turned on his stomach and studied the little ferns that grew all about them around the trees. Where they grew the ground was soft and porous, springy with dead fronds. He scraped about with a dead fern stick. Then he sat back and looked up at the green roof above. At last he gave Richard a push.

Richard groaned, swallowed, and sat up. "What's the matter? What's happened?" He was ready to spring to his feet.

"Nothing," said Peter. "That's the trouble."

"What do you mean—nothing?"

"Well, nothing. Listen." They sat silent, listening, and Prue, who had woken at the voices, listened too.

"I can't hear anything," said Richard.

"That's what I mean—nothing. Wouldn't you think there'd be a few birds? This is the time they sing."

For a long time they did not say anything. One by one they lifted their heads and gazed into the branches. There was no movement at all up there, and in the whole of the forest there was not a single sound.

" 'Member I said last night there weren't any ants?" said Peter. "Well, there aren't. Have you ever been in a place where there weren't any ants? And there aren't any other insects—or grubs or anything. That's why it's so quiet. There's *nothing.*"

All of them, sitting there, began to feel a cold chill spreading like a curse through the whole of their bodies. At last Richard said, "Insecticides. Maybe this place is completely polluted. Maybe it's poisoned. We ought to get out."

"The trees are growing," said Prue.

"That's all that is growing," said Peter. "Not another thing."

"Except—" said Richard, and stopped.

"Except what? Except what, Richard?"

After a long pause Richard said, "Except that I wonder if they used too much poison. I mean—they poisoned themselves as well. That's why the forest's just been left—like this."

"Then where are the bones?" said Peter. He spoke in a thin, unnatural voice.

"The bones could have been eaten away by the poison," said Richard.

It was Prue who broke the evil spell. "I don't believe it," she said, and her voice was the only one with its natural ring. "I don't believe anything's been poisoned. It's just that—" She swallowed. "What I think is there never has been anything here. There never have been birds or insects or animals. Just trees. Always just trees."

There was a long silence, and not one of them could tell if he were relieved or not. It was the desolation, the resounding emptiness of the forest that penetrated to their bones—that filled them with a cold dread. Suddenly Richard jumped up. "I don't like it," he said. "I don't like it at all. Let's get out. Come on. Quick. Let's get out." He looked rather wildly about him. The long colonnades were empty. The small ferns hung motionless in the rays of the early sun. Nothing stirred. "Let's go to the lake," he shouted. "Come on. Run."

They did not know why they ran. There seemed no danger anywhere. The peace in the forest was absolute. But Prue and Peter could feel with Richard that in this kind of life, this kind of silent, static growing, they had no place, any more than they had had a place on the lava ridge. They made for the lake, pelting through the forest, kicking the small ferns and tussocks as they ran, crushing and bruising them in a way they had never been crushed or bruised before. They could still hear the splashing of the waves, and they made for the sound, desperate, now that they had started, to get out from under the canopy of ferns. To reach the open sky was all they wanted.

They came to the edge of the lake more suddenly than they expected, for here, far from the ridge, out on the flat plain, the forest came right down to the edge of the water. They burst through a grove of saplings, a comforting sight, for they looked just like the tree ferns they were all accustomed to, and found themselves at the water's edge. Great waves were rolling up the earthy bank, tossing clouds of spray against the tree trunks and damping the fronds above. As far as they could see the surface of the lake was in a state of wild upheaval with big waves rolling, it seemed, in all directions. But they could not see far, because a fog rose up from the water, blotting out the sky and concealing all but their immediate surroundings. Somewhere far out in the fog a white and silent shape drifted by and a draft of cold air reached them from the water. Prue moved close to Richard and clutched him by the sleeve. He whispered in her ear, "It's all right. It's only an iceberg."

Peter took a step forward, bent down, and when the next wave splashed up near his feet put his fingers in the water. He looked around quickly. "It's quite hot," he said.

They did not know what to do next. Now that they were here, the lake was as repellent as the forest. And they had a feeling that at any moment it might develop some new and unexpected danger. The water might grow hotter still, the waves might engulf the forest. Now, at the water's edge, they could go neither forward nor back. Richard made the first move.

"We'll have to go along the edge of the lake. Between the water and the trees. I'll lead the way. Come on." He started off and they followed, skirting the tree roots on one side, skipping back to avoid the waves on the other.

Over the forest the sun still shone, and they walked through patches of brightness. At these times they could see the sky and although it was a strange color—a lurid pinky-yellow rather than the clear blue they knew—it was a comfort to them. But more often the mists from the lake blotted it out, and they walked in a sodden gloom that smelled faintly of fish and decay. It was offensive but less ominous than yesterday's disgusting smell of sulphur. They walked for many hours, and the lake thrashed and rolled and roared on their left-hand side.

It was perhaps early afternoon when Prue said, "The waves are getting bigger."

They stopped and looked out across the lake and all saw that the waves were mountainous and more chaotic than ever, heaving up and sucking away to leave gaping hollows in the surface. The color had changed to a murky, muddy brown that was quite opaque. The mist was growing thicker.

"It's not all waves," said Peter at last. "There's something in it. Look. Over there."

"Don't be ridiculous," said Richard. He bent down and felt the water. "It's too hot. No fish could live in that."

84

"Perhaps that's why," said Prue, and a shiver went through them all.

"There!" shouted Peter suddenly. "See?"

A mountainous wave had just receded at the edge of the mist, leaving a swirling whirlpool. As they watched, something rose in the middle of the whirlpool—something curved, shining, and gunmetal gray. Involuntarily they all took a step backward. It subsided again, but they could not take their eyes from the spot where it had vanished. Another wave rolled over and the whirlpool dissolved. Then Richard gave a shout and pointed, speechless. Nearer at hand the gray thing was rising again. Except that it was smooth and shining, it might have been a submarine. It rose higher, slid forward, and as it vanished a great fish tail came out of the water, slapped on the surface and disappeared.

"A whale," shouted Peter.

But it had not seemed just like a whale, and as they watched, it surfaced again—this time nearer still, and a strongly fishy smell swept across the water, which heaved and bubbled. A spume of spray was tossed into the air, and suddenly a kind of head emerged, and the great mouth was open, water streaming from between the rows of teeth. Near the top of the head tiny eyes gleamed. They just had time to see the red, gaping throat before it disappeared, and they saw, as the rest of the great body slid through the water, that it was making for the shore. The direction in which it was swimming would bring it to within some yards of where they stood.

"Quick," said Richard. "Run."

They began to run but pulled up short. In the lake ahead of them another gray shape was surfacing, surging frantically through the water. And near it, another—and another. The water began to boil with the heaving backs of desperate monsters. And every so often a head with the same rows of savage teeth would rise into the mist, and a flail-like tail would crash onto the surface with a noise like a gun. And they were all making for the shore, racing like torpedoes through the water.

"What shall we do?" said Prue.

"We can only keep running," Richard shouted back to her.

They flew on around the edge of the lake. It was hard to watch their feet and the approaching creatures at the same time. There remained still escape through the forest, but the forest was inimical and while they could stay under the open sky, they tried desperately to do so. They began to spread out, Richard ahead, then Peter, light and wiry, then Prue, and every so often as she ran, she looked behind. Once she jumped sideways because at her very feet the great snout and gleaming teeth of one of the creatures rose up from the water, and all around it the water frothed. She tried to shout for help, but she had no breath, and even if she had, the boys would not have heard above the sound of the waves. She thought she would be forced into the forest, losing sight of them and being lost to them when they came to look for her. Ahead the stretch of shore between her and Peter was widening, and the tumultuous waters told her that soon a number of the creatures would be struggling to land. She began to feel she was lost, and her lungs were forcing her tortured breath faster than it could flow, when she became aware that her right hand, which had been clenched beside her, was being forced open and another hand slipped into it, holding it, grasping it, pulling her along. And the hand that held her was large and strong, and strength and comfort flowed from its palm up her arm and through her down to her very feet. Her breathing became easier, her stride grew longer and her muscles began to work smoothly, strongly, and tirelessly. With her hand still clasped, she found herself flying over the ground, catching up with the boys without effort.

She reached Peter first, and he glanced around as she came up. Without speaking, he took her other hand and they ran on together. When they drew level with Richard, Prue tried to shout to Peter to take his hand, but it was not necessary. Peter flung out his left hand, grabbing at Richard's, and they went on together, the three of them, hand in hand. And always Prue felt herself held and given strength by the great hand that clasped her own. It was not necessary to look round. She knew there was nothing to see.

After that their fear left them. The danger, if danger it had been, fell behind, and they ran on and the lake slipped by on their left-hand side and the forest on their right. Their way was decided for them and they did not have to think. They ran in a dream, and time and the land slid away beneath their feet. It might have been day or night; they did not know, and it did not matter. The running—the effortless running—was all.

Some hours—or was it years?—later they found themselves sitting on a green, sweet-smelling bank. Many little low plants were growing on it, and it was these, crushed by their bodies, that produced the fresh, clean smell of herbs. Growing with the plants was grass, luxuriant, but of a curious kind. The blades had a feathery look. Together, the grass and the little plants made a comfortable bed, and they lay back on the slope, gazing into the sky. To their relief the strange lurid colors had gone, and they saw only a clear, deep blue that seemed very far away and innocent. The air about them was crisp and cool, and the lake at the bottom of the slope was gleaming placidly in the sunshine. Behind them a forest of pines and certain deciduous trees covered the rolling countryside. From where they sat, they could smell the warm, resinous sap. It was all very familiar and comforting. They experienced a sense of well-being and good health partly caused by relief and partly by the certain knowledge that they were safe at last.

[10]

FOR A LONG TIME THEY lay and chewed the feathery blades of grass and gazed at the sky, and it seemed too much effort to say anything at all. At last Richard said, "I still can't understand what happened. Why were we able to run so fast? How did we know where to go? And how far have we come? Did someone help us?"

This was the question Prue had been hoping he would not ask. She looked at Peter now, wishing he would have an answer. But he only said, "Prue helped me. She held my hand."

"Well, who helped Prue? She wasn't strong enough to help us all. She was the slowest. She was the last." His voice held an edge of anger, and Prue knew she would have to say something. Richard liked to have answers, and there had been too many things since the car got washed away that had not been explained to him. Now, feeling that she and Peter must be holding something back, he was becoming resentful. She knew her explanation would not satisfy him, but she would have to speak.

Reluctantly she said, "You see, she came and held my hand."

"She? Who? We haven't seen a soul since those Aborigines." He turned swiftly to Peter "Have you, Peter? Did you see anybody?"

"Not 'she'," said Peter. "Him."

"*What* him? What are you talking about?"

"Him. You know. Him who always comes." Peter sounded slightly impatient.

Prue now looked at him in amazement. "Did you—Peter, did you see her too? And the voice? I thought it was me—inside me. Did you hear the voice too?"

"Not her—him," said Peter crossly. "Well, I always hear him, don't I? He's always about."

"What in the name of heaven are you talking about?" They both jumped because Richard had shouted. He looked from one to the other of them, and his baffled anger was growing. "Prue, you're older than Peter. Just, for the love of Mike, tell me what you're both talking about."

"Yes." She felt suddenly sorry for Richard because it must seem to him that they were talking in riddles, family secrets that deliberately excluded him. But it was not like this at all. She was floundering almost as much as he, with the one big difference that she was prepared to accept what she could not understand. She could live along without always needing an answer. And Peter was different too. He had not yet learned to expect answers for everything. He flowed happily with the current. She had no answer now, and she could only tell him what she knew. "I first heard this voice," she said tentatively.

"What voice?" said Richard sharply. "When? You never told me."

"I didn't think you'd believe me. Besides, I didn't know if it was a voice. I thought it might just be me."

"I can't understand," said Richard, and threw himself on his stomach on the grass. "I can't understand a word you're saying. First it's a voice, and then it isn't, and then you think it was your own. WHAT ARE YOU TRYING TO TELL ME?" The last words were shouted, and then he dropped his head into his crooked arms.

Prue moved toward him, put a hand on his back, and bent down. "You see, Richard," she said into his ear. "I don't *know* what it is. I'm trying to tell you just what happened. You did ask." She sat back on her heels, waiting for him to say something.

Peter got up and wandered off. The conversation had ceased to have anything to do with him, and he never liked cross voices. Richard lifted his head to look at her. "Go on," he said. "I'll try not to interrupt."

"You remember when we were in the gully when the fire came?" He nodded. "It happened first then, when I was lying in the creek and I couldn't dig the hole. Then—" She thought for a moment. "Yes. Then it came when we saw the Aborigines. It said to be gentle and not to be afraid. And, Richard—" She drew in a long, slow breath and leaned toward him. "Always, whenever it spoke, it was like being taken care of. It was like—being minded, so you couldn't be afraid any more because you

90

knew that however things were it was all right."

He said nothing, for he knew she was speaking the truth, but his eyes were still on her face. She went on. "The next time was up on that dreadful ridge, with the lava and the volcano. She came in the mist. Richard, I saw her." She stopped.

"What was she like?" said Richard at last.

Immediately Prue looked puzzled. "I don't know. Like mist. Like mist and the sun. And she bent over me. Then I knew it was all right. And I knew we had to go down the slope. Before she came I heard her—or someone— saying, 'Run, run,' but when she came, she didn't speak. But I knew."

Richard drew in his breath and put his hand over hers. "Oh, Prue," was all he said.

"Then—then it was the hand. When I couldn't run any more and I didn't know what to do. The hand came and held mine. And it was all right."

"What did she look like then?" said Richard.

"That's the funny part. She came and held my hand, but she really wasn't there. There was nothing to see at all. It didn't seem to matter. I knew it would be all right." She stopped because there was no more to say.

When it was clear that she had come to the end, Richard said, "But that doesn't explain it at all. It doesn't tell me anything. What *happened?* That's what I want to know."

She shook her head. "I knew it wouldn't satisfy you. You mustn't ask me for explanations. There aren't any."

"Explanations are the only things that matter. Can't you see?"

She could only shake her head again. "They don't

seem to matter at all when all you want is to be looked after," she said finally.

He sat up now and turned toward her, putting his hands on her shoulders and pulling her toward him so that he could study her face. "Prue," he said quietly, "does your head still ache?"

She nodded. "Not now, but then—on the ridge. It ached like anything."

"My poor Prue," he said. "We must look after you. I should have known that after the accident. I should have made you rest and not expected you to have come so far. Prue, lie down and rest now. Try to sleep. I'll stay awake and watch." He pressed her gently to the grass, pulled off his shirt, rolled it into a ball, and put it under her head.

Prue obediently lay down, turned away from him and closed her eyes. There was no need for him to know that they had stupidly filled with tears. She saw that this was to be his explanation. She knew he was wrong, but now he would accept no other. For a time she pretended to sleep. She heard Peter come back and heard Richard whisper that he was to be quiet, for she was not well and had to sleep. She heard Peter say in his normal voice, "Prue's never sick." Richard said, "Shut up," angrily, and there was silence. But she was not tired, and she could not sleep, and she wanted very much to say something that would make Richard happy. So after what seemed a suitable time, she sat up again as if she had just woken.

"I expect Mummy will be looking after Aunt Kate just like you're looking after me. I expect she has her all tucked up in bed telling her not to worry because we're sure to turn up. Won't they be glad to see us again?" Her words brought the familiar things of home rushing back into their minds. It came as a surprise to them all how long it was since they had thought of home.

"Your flat'll be empty," said Peter. "I 'spect somebody'll go in to dust it and clean the bath."

"Nobody'll be using the bath," said Prue, without thinking.

But Richard, whom it was meant to cheer, said, "Do you think we'll ever get home? I lost the way home a long time ago."

"We'll find the way home one day," said Prue with confidence.

"I don't know," said Richard. "I don't know any more. And if we do, how do I know Mother will be there? And if she isn't, what'll I do with the flat? What'll I do with my life?" His voice rose, and suddenly he buried his face in his hands.

"You'll be an engineer, of course," said Peter. "An' I'll come an' live with you in the flat, Richard. I like your flat."

"Shut up, Peter," said Prue in her turn. But she added for Richard's sake, "You won't be able to. Aunt Kate'll go back as soon as Richard gets home."

The best of the day was past now, and as the sun began to go down, they could feel the first touch of frost in the air. Prue shook out Richard's shirt and handed it to him. "Put it on, Richard," she said. "It's going to be cold tonight."

The light was leaving the lake, and the shadows of the pines behind them had long since driven the sun from their bank. "What do we do now?" said Richard. "Where do we go?"

"Somewhere warm for the night," said Peter promptly. "It's too cold here."

So they got up and made their way toward the trees, and the smell of the pines soothed them and made them feel at home. They did not have to go very far into the forest before they found a sheltered place in among the roots of one of the big trees. The ground was thickly covered with pine needles and soft to lie on. Richard gathered some dead branches that had fallen from the trees and erected a kind of cover, and they crawled in among the dry pine needles and curled up, pressing together for warmth. Strangely, the thought of danger did not occur to any of them, and they slept peacefully until the morning.

They woke to find the sun sparkling on the frosty ground. The lake shone and the trees basked in the sun, exuding their resinous smell as they grew warmer.

"It feels like a holiday," said Peter, and ran out of the trees into the sunshine.

It felt like a holiday to all of them, and as they no longer knew which way to go and for some reason felt reluctant to go anywhere for the moment, they remained where they were. For three days they stayed in that place, drinking the crisp lake water and eating nuts and berries that they found in the forest. Oddly, they felt no hunger at any time except when there was food to eat. Then they ate it with relish. Richard usually had some doubts about whether they would all end up poisoned, but Peter told him that if it tasted nice it was all right, and Prue said that if you tried a little bit first you would be quite safe. At any rate they felt no ill effects, and they filled in the days happily exploring their immediate surroundings.

At first they thought they were once again in a countryside they knew and understood. They knew about pine trees, and if these were a slightly different shape from the ones they were accustomed to, at least they grew in the same way, and their regular rings of symmetrical branches reminded them of some they had seen in pictures. It was the same with many of the deciduous trees that grew among them. The straight, smooth trunks and the pale green, heart-shaped leaves were familiar, too. And near the lake where there seemed to be marshes, there were thickets of palm trees, and a different kind of pine with a more feathery top. But none of them resembled the fern-like trees of the last horrifying forest they had been in. More reassuring still, there were insects and some little, scurrying animals that Richard thought might be rats or mice. There were lizards, too, of varying sizes and rather unusual shapes and a few birds, which Peter had at first mistaken for lizards. They could not see the birds very well, for they were high in the trees and there were not very many of them, but they were able to fly, so they must have been birds.

"Naturally," said Richard, "you can't expect to find exactly the same kind of animals everywhere. They are sure to vary with the kind of country they live in. They have to adapt."

There were fish in the lake, too, for several times they saw them rise out in the deeper water.

So for three days they were at peace and happy. Running along the edge of the lake, tramping through the bracken at the edge of the forest, they forgot their anxieties and the need to go home and laughed and played and explored. And Richard shed his fears and whistled as he went.

95

11

IT WAS ON THE FOURTH DAY that Peter climbed the pine tree and came down again to say that something funny was going on at the head of the lake.

"What do you mean—something funny?" said Richard.

"I don't know. But something's moving. Something big." For once Peter's confidence was jolted.

Together they went to the edge of the lake and looked in the direction of the marshes. The land flattened out at that westward end of the lake, and they had seen what looked like thickets of reed and low palms. But they had not explored far in that direction because it had looked dull and unattractive. Now they stared at the dark green line of vegetable growth. "Nothing's different," said Richard at last.

"You can't see it except from higher," said Peter.

"Climb the tree, Richard, and have a look," said Prue.

"Very well. But I'll bet it's nothing."

"This tree, Richard," said Peter, who had climbed most of them. "This is easiest."

"I'll choose my own tree, thanks," said Richard.

Richard climbed until he was about half way up. Then he stopped, moved out on to a branch that overhung the lake, and sat for a time looking at the marshes. Then he climbed down. Prue and Peter were waiting at the bottom. His face was puzzled. "There's something there, all right. Probably been there all the time and we never would have seen it if Peter hadn't climbed his tree. I think it's just a mound of mud. Goodness knows why there's nothing growing on it. But mud is what it looks like. Matter of fact, there seem to be several and all of them are bare. Probably clay or something."

"Then how could it move?" said Peter. "I saw it moving."

Richard looked hard at him. "You couldn't have," he said.

"Well, I did, see. You don't have to believe me." And Peter stamped off.

"How could they have moved?" said Richard indignantly to Prue.

All the rest of that day they kept glancing toward the head of the lake, and that night they barricaded themselves more firmly in their hollow among the tree roots, and none of them slept as well as they had before.

No one mentioned the strange mounds next morning, and everyone tried hard to avoid looking toward the marshes. But about midday Peter disappeared for a short time and reappeared rather white about the face. He walked straight up to Richard.

"The mounds have gone," he said. "So they must have moved."

Richard said nothing, but he ran to the nearest tree, swung himself into the lower branches, and began to climb. After a few moments he was back again, and his face was as white as Peter's. "From now on," he said, as he picked himself up, for he had jumped down rather hurriedly, "From now on, we must keep a watch. Peter, you and I will take it in turns to sit up in the tree. And the other two must stay within earshot."

The sun still shone, the insects still made their strange little whirring noises, and the lake still lapped peacefully against the grassy bank. But the happiness of the last three days had gone. They amused themselves about the open slope and made short excursions into the forest, but they were constantly alert for a shout from the tree and their minds were never at rest. To Prue the only good thing about those last two days was that Richard was once again in command. This was the normal, homely pattern, and it seemed to her right and proper.

When it came it was not, in fact, a shout as they had expected. Peter was on watch, and he surprised them by sliding quickly down the tree, dropping to the ground from a higher branch than he usually chose, and rushing to where Richard was sitting dabbling his bare feet in the lake. He tugged at his shirt. "Quick, Richard. Come and look. Come up the tree. Quick."

"What is it?" Richard jumped up and spoke as he ran.

"Don't know," panted Peter as he ran behind him. "It's just—funny."

Richard swung himself into the branches, and Peter climbed up behind him. He pointed out across the lake. "See those sort of palms over there? On the other side of the lake? Watch them."

While they watched in silence, Prue came to the foot of the tree. Suddenly, alone on the ground, she felt afraid.

"There!" shouted Peter. "There. See?"

After a long time Richard said, "Good God!" Twisting around on his branch to say something to Peter, he saw Prue clinging to the trunk behind him.

"I couldn't wait down there," she said. "Not alone. Where is it? Let me see."

Richard pointed to the palm grove, and it was waving

about as if a gale had suddenly risen on that side of the lake. The long palm fronds swayed and tossed. And then, as they watched, something long, gray, and sinuous rose from among the green. A small, pear-shaped nob on the end of it hovered over the palms, and then the gray tube arched, and the bulbous end of it plunged into the branches, and when it rose again, it seemed that some of the branches rose with it. At such a distance it was hard to see clearly, but Richard suddenly shouted, "It's a head. It's a head on a long neck. I think it's tearing at the palm trees."

Then, as they watched, a whole clump of palms swayed and bowed to the ground, and a huge gray shape surged over the top of it, pressing the palms flat to the earth.

"Golly!" said Peter. And then he said, "I've saw that thing somewhere before. It's real all right. Golly."

Prue said, and she could not keep the quiver out of her voice, "It's a picture in one of your books at home. But the book said it had been dead for years and years."

"Well, it isn't," said Peter, " 'cos there it is. What'll we do, Richard?"

Before he could reply, a further area of palms began to thrash about. Three more colossal gray shapes loomed out from among them, and three more long gray necks carried their tiny heads to the farthest tips of the palms. Even as they watched, the palms on the edge of the lake became violently agitated, heeled over, crashed down, and one after another the massive gray bodies emerged at the water's edge. One after another the gray necks uncoiled, stretched themselves out, and lowered their heads to the water.

"They've come for a drink," said Peter. In their tree the three of them were motionless. Then Peter said again, "What'll we do, Richard?"

Before Richard could answer one of the creatures raised its head on the long neck high in the air. They could see the strange mouth open and then heard a high, clear whistle. Carried over the water, its pitch and volume were tremendous. Two more of the creatures raised their heads, and twice more they heard the loud whistle. When their vibrations died away, the silence flowed back, deep and still. Then it seemed that far away across the lake the whole of the rolling green landscape became agitated. The vegetation as far as they could see boiled with heaving gray backs, all converging on the group by the lake. It was like a range of hills on the move.

"What'll we do, Richard?" This time it was a frantic shout.

"What can we do?" This time Richard turned to look at him. "You can't run away from a thing that size. If they want to do us harm they will. We can't stop them."

"We could hide," said Peter.

But Prue said, "If they're eating those palm trees, they're probably not carn—carn—"

"Carnivorous," said Richard. "Perhaps not. And perhaps they won't cross the lake. We may be safest where we are."

"Can't we go into the forest?" said Peter.

"Maybe tomorrow, when there's light. Once we go in among the trees, we can't see anything. It's better to stay where we can watch them."

"I don't like it," said Peter, and his voice was a wail.

"None of us likes it," said Prue. "But Richard's right. We'll do what he says."

100

The afternoon was dying, and the light was beginning to fade. None of them liked the idea of the night to come. They remained in the tree and watched for as long as they could see. There were a number of the enormous creatures at the lake's edge now, and they were alternately lowering their heads to drink and tearing at the palms. Every so often one raised its head to utter again that clear whistle. Little by little they were moving along the edge of the water, tearing, chewing, and drinking as they went.

"Don't they ever sleep?" said Peter, when the last of the daylight had gone and they could no longer see the heaving gray backs. "How can we sleep if they don't? I'm getting tired."

"We'll have to," said Richard. "We'll hide somewhere among the trees. And we'll keep watch. We'll take it in turns, one by one. And we'd better remember—" He stopped and glanced across the lake. "We'd better remember that sound carries over water. We'd better keep as quiet as we can."

They climbed down from the tree and felt very helpless and exposed once they were on the ground. But it was reassuring to have Richard in charge again, and as he pointed out, they were no safer in the tree, for they could be plucked off the topmost branches as easily as off the ground. It was consolation in a way, and for the time being, it was all they had. Prue and Peter followed Richard into the forest, and this time they found themselves a tree whose exposed roots were bigger and more concealing. Their sleeping place was less comfortable, but nobody felt like complaining. By the time they had settled down it was deep night and quite dark. The forest was very quiet, and their ears were strained to hear any sound that came across the lake. Once or twice they fancied they could hear splashing, but the sound never increased, and they heard no more of the strange whistles. The first watch was considered the easiest and safest, and Peter was put on this because Richard thought he was less likely to fall asleep now than later.

In fact, they all remained awake for the whole of Peter's watch, for sleep, when ears are strained to hear and muscles are tensed for action, is not easy to achieve. The watches were changed by guesswork. And they took their turns and the night wore on. And nothing happened to disturb their rest. But when the first breaths of pre-dawn wind began to stir the treetops and there was that first feeling of transparency in the darkness, a kind of relief flowed through them all, and the two not on watch fell into their first deep sleep, and Richard, who was the watchman, did not know when the eyelids came down over his eyes. He did not know when his body slipped into a sitting position and relaxed in sleep.

For a time the new day grew undisturbed. Over the lake the light flowered and grew bright. The slight frost became drops of dew and dissolved in vapor, and the first insects began to stir and creak.

This was how it was when Peter woke. He saw that the others were asleep, saw that Richard, the watchman, had slid, relaxed, to the foot of the tree, and realized that they had been unguarded for some time. He did not move but lay still and watchful, ears alert and only his eyes moving as he carefully searched the glade.

It was his ears that told him why he had woken. The whistling had begun again. This time one whistle did not answer another in a kind of courteous reptilian repartee as they had the evening before. This time they all struck up at once. And the sound shrilled piercingly into the morning air. He remained motionless, but gradually all the muscles of his body tensed themselves. It was vital to know where the whistling was coming from. If it was from across the water, the creatures were far away. If it was not—he knew they dared not move until they knew. He looked at Prue and Richard. Both were still deeply asleep, and both were still partially concealed by the spreading tree roots. Without a sound he moved out from beneath the tree.

Carefully he went from tree trunk to tree trunk, from bush to bush until he reached the lakeside. It lay glassy and serene before him, the last mists of night dissolving above the surface. The farther shore stood out sharp and clear below the fading wisps of vapor. Nothing moved there at all. But the whistling continued, and there was a note in it now that set his nerves twanging. Fear is easily communicated. But there was nothing to be seen, and he was not sure where the sound came from. It cut the tranquil morning from all points of the compass. Suddenly, after one quick look behind he ran to the tree they had climbed the day before and swung himself quickly to the top. To the right he could see a long way down the lake, where the wreathing mist still hid the shore. On his left he could see as far as the end of the lake and the marshes that terminated it. The palms, their feathery tops catching the first gleams of sun, appeared to be as motionless as the lake. The marshes steamed a little as they grew warmer. But there were no gray mounds and nothing moved. The pitch of the whistling was rising and it rang in his skull like a fever. He wanted to scream.

Suddenly his self-control deserted him. He slid to the foot of the tree and ran with his hands over his ears into the forest.

It was not necessary for him to speak. Prue and Richard, woken brusquely from sleep, heard the whistling at once and needed only to look at his face.

"Where is it?" said Richard. Peter shook his head. His lips were pressed so tightly that the blood had been driven from them. After one sharp look, Richard ran without thought of caution to the lake. When Prue and Peter found him, he was already sliding down their lookout tree to the ground. The whistling was everywhere, shrill and unbearable.

"Can't see anything," he shouted. "Not a thing. But they must have gone down there." He pointed to the far reaches of the lake, still hidden in mist. "That's the only part we can't see, and that's the way they were going last night. Come on. We'd better go this way—and fast." They followed him because he had made a decision and because he was already on his way to the head of the lake, to the steaming marshes and the palm groves.

The whistling accompanied them. Once or twice as they ran, they thought it had changed direction, and now and then it grew fainter, as if the creatures were moving farther off. But they could never pinpoint the sound, and after each period of fading, it grew louder than ever.

They had been plunging through one of the thicker parts of the forest, glad of the brief concealment of the trees, when they suddenly emerged into the open. The ground sloped sharply at their feet, and before them, for mile on mile, stretched the marsh, a vast area of unstable mud. As far as they could see, the mud was dotted with tufted grasses, small ferns, and stands of bamboo-like plants. These had feathery leaves at regular intervals up the tubular stems. They were everywhere in clumps six feet high. Beyond them, farther off and perhaps on patches of drier ground, were the palm groves—areas of fluffy emerald green in the distance.

They slid down the slope, hoping that the clumps of grass and the wiry fern stems would be strong enough to hold them, and for perhaps a hundred yards it seemed that this might be so. Then they found the black mud sucking around their ankles, pulling at their shoes, while the vegetable growth they had depended on sank beneath their feet. They were enveloped in a putrid smell, and a multitude of tiny insects, disturbed by their progress, rose up around them and settled, stinging, on their faces. Richard, who was leading, took a step that submerged him to the knees, dragged himself backward and shouted, "Back! Go back, or we'll never get out."

With difficulty they retreated, reached the foot of the slope, and climbed up it. They brushed the insects from their faces and began to scrape the black mud from their feet and legs. They found themselves glad of the great tree trunks at their backs. The whistling was louder than ever and more frenzied. Then Prue felt her shoulder clutched, felt the nails dig in, and saw that Peter, crowding to her side, was pointing with his other hand out across the marsh.

"Look," he whispered. "Prue, look."

In the distance the tops of the palm trees were swaying. A kind of miasma rose far out on the marsh, and before they saw anything at all, they knew that somewhere out there, where they had been trying to go, the whole area was full of violent movement. Then the edge of the palm grove became wildly agitated, bent, swept the ground, and out from it burst two, three, six—ten of the great creatures they had seen the previous day. They saw now why they had not noticed them sooner. The sinuous gray necks were stretched horizontal, the little reptilian heads straining forward. They were stretched low to the ground in flight, and as they thundered out from the palms, their mouths were wide open, and from them issued the terrible whistling. Out they came, surging from the trampled palms on to the marsh. And as they plunged through the stands of bamboo-like plants and over the sea of little ferns and grasses, mud and water rose up around them, and the sound of their great feet, dragged from the sucking mud, was like pistol shots. In no more than a few minutes the marsh became a raging bedlam. They were more clearly visible now. They had great, reptilian tails, long, crooked hind legs, and the front feet, raised together from time to time as the creatures leaned back to drag them from the mud, were clawed and much smaller than the hind feet. Here and there, as they crossed the treacherous surface, one blundered into a softer patch and its body suddenly sank deep, the small front feet clawed at the ground ahead, and then all vanished. And the last to go was the head and neck, straining vertically upward, mouth wide and forked tongue flickering, sinking slowly into the depths of the marsh.

But many survived. Before them the stick-like plants went over, were bent flat, and submerged in the mud. Here and there water splashed. Now and then a spout of mud rose into the air, and the smell of putrefying vegetable matter spread over the surface of the marsh. The

106

flattened bamboo-like stems provided a firmer surface, and the creatures began to travel more quickly.

"They're coming this way," screamed Peter. "They're coming toward us." And he flung his arms around Prue's waist.

"Come back!" shouted Richard, who had already reached the trees. "Hurry."

But Prue could not move. Her legs seemed frozen to the ground. She staggered as Peter flung himself upon her, and she was helpless. And then, as she stood there, she saw a great figure burst out from among the distant palms; a figure quite as large as but different from the others that surged over the boggy ground. This seemed clad in armor-plating. Its backbone and huge tail were ridged with fins, beginning with the dorsal, the biggest of all. Its neck was shorter, its head much, much bigger, and its gaping mouth showed two rows of savage teeth. This was what they ran from. This was what had harried them, up and down, since dawn. It rushed now toward a fleeing group of the first creatures, its great head lunging and grabbing. The sound of its snapping teeth rose clear above the whistling, and when it lifted its head, the jaws ran red. The heads of the other creatures now became frenzied, waving in all directions, and their movements became even more agitated and frantic. Then, as the new monster's head dived again, Prue saw one of them roll over, heard the whistle turn to a kind of shriek, while two enormous hind legs rose into the air and its head sank, pressed into the enveloping mud. Immediately the finned monster dived upon it, tearing with its teeth and pounding with its strong front feet. All around it the other creatures fled away and the vanguard—much closer to the children now—pounded their way over the quaking clumps of grass and caked with mud approached the short, steep slope where Prue and Peter still stood locked together. About the stricken monster a patch of gleaming red spread out over the grass and turned the ferns from emerald green to crimson.

"Come *on*," shouted Richard again, and his voice cracked.

But now the finned monster left its prey and, in a series of bounding plunges, came after the rest of them. They could see the tiny, bulging eyes of the victims crazed with fear. Prue felt herself grasped roughly around the waist and pulled off her feet. Richard dragged her to the shelter of the nearest tree. She had Peter by the hand, and they tumbled in among the great roots as the whistling filled the forest, deafening, piercing, agonized, and agonizing. A sudden growl broke through the whistling, and they saw the toothed monster catch up with the hindmost of the others. They saw it tear away with streaming jaws a piece of pink and quivering flesh. The victim gave one scream and sank back from the slope. Its great weight pressed it down, grass, ferns and all, deeper and deeper into the mud. Above it the great jaws worked and a pair of expressionless eyes gleamed like steel.

The three children clung together, cowering at the foot of the tree. The creatures were all around them now, like thunder in the air above, and the attacker was climbing up the slope. Something enormous, gray, and reeking of putrefaction towered above them. The tree staggered, groaned, and beneath their feet the great roots heaved and strained. Out of the bedlam Prue heard a voice say, "Stay together. Only stay together." The tree shuddered, creaking, and one by one the roots exploded out of the ground. The whole spreading, underground system that bore the soaring branches heaved beneath them. Above, the gray body lurched as a gigantic hind claw scrabbled for purchase just beside them, and they felt themselves falling—deep into the great hole left by the tree's roots. Down they went, down into the darkness, clutched together, holding tight, having nothing but each other to cling to, and gradually the turmoil faded, the whistling died away, and they came imperceptibly to rest. Prue could not have said why, but she knew that what she clung to had been neither Richard nor Peter.

For a long time none of them moved. They lay, half stunned, with closed eyes, and now she knew that the bodies beside her, to whom she still clung, were those of the two boys. The words, "stay together," still reverberated faintly in her memory, and it seemed, as she lay motionless, that the words changed. They said, "Why did you stay so long? You should have gone on." And, growing louder, the words, "gone on—gone on," rang like a gong in her head. She felt a body wriggle beside her, and she opened her eyes and found it was Peter. But it was not he who had spoken.

They were all three lying on dry grass in the midst of a great expanse of rolling country. Behind them was a grove of saplings that swayed in the gentle breeze. As they swayed, they rubbed together, and perhaps it was the saplings that were sounding that deep, repeated note. But Prue turned to look and saw that their protector stood among the young trees.

12

THE BRANCHES STILL WAVED about his head, and his legs were lost among the stems of the young trees. He could have been any age at all. She saw now that he was a man, for the face was firm, brown, and square, and although its expression was gentle, there was no softness in it. His body seemed to be clad loosely in some rough, brown garment that hung about among the encircling leaves and appeared almost part of them. His feet were bare, brown, and muscular like the roots of trees and seemed as firmly fixed on the ground. His eyes were bright, as if the sun shone through them from behind. It was a figure such as she had never seen and yet—it was as familiar to her as home. She had never seen it, but she had never been absent from it. Here, no matter where home might be, was where she belonged.

"Thank you," she said lifting her head and looking into his face.

A smile broke across it, and he said, "My children, you delayed too long."

She had forgotten Richard, but she suddenly heard his voice. "What's happening? Prue, who are you talking to?" He was standing beside her, peering into her face. His own was full of alarm and suspicion.

"Can't you see him, Richard?" She pulled him around to face their protector, but now she discovered that perhaps he was not easy to see, for his body had somehow become confused with the stems and branches he stood among.

"I can't see anything but a clump of saplings," said

110

Richard. He noticed Peter lying on the grass beside him and said, "Can you see anything, Peter?"

Peter was making a circle of round, white pebbles, and he glanced up and then down again. "Only what was there before," he said. "What's always there."

"Prue," Richard took her by the arm, led her to the patch of shade made by the saplings, and pulled her to the ground. "Rest here," he said. "Sit down and rest here for a while."

She was sitting at the very feet of their protector, and she had never felt so contented in her life. But it was time Richard should accept the truth. "I am *not* sick, Richard," she said. "My headache has gone. And we have been saved. How do you think we got away? How do you think we got here if we weren't saved?"

He knelt down beside her. "Prue, you aren't well. You must be careful. Somehow, I've got to get you home." He emphasized the last word.

Before she thought, Prue said, "I am home."

A spasm crossed Richard's face, and he leaned toward her. "That's what I mean. You think these things. You think or imagine all sorts of things. But they're not true. This isn't home, Prue. How can you think so? Surely you haven't forgotten your own house? Remember your mother's hens? And that terrible cat your father calls Fluff? Remember the big gum tree by the gate? Prue—" He took her by the arm and almost shook it. "Do you remember our flat, right on the top of the building? You haven't forgotten your Aunt Kate? We have to go home and find her. We have to make sure she's all right. How do I know, out here, wherever we are, what's happened to my mother? I've got to find out.

We've got to find our way home." He was not instructing her any longer. He was pleading with her, and she could only say, "Yes, I know. I understand, Richard. I do remember. And we are trying to find our way home. That's all we've ever been doing."

A voice behind her said, "You are all on your way home. When you have learned to know me, you will have come home. Peter knows me because he has not yet had time to forget me." There was a pause. Above their heads the leaves rustled. Peter was still playing with his pebbles. Richard sat uneasily, looking from Prue to Peter and then to the saplings. He knew, at least, that whatever it was that held Prue's attention was somewhere among them.

Prue said tentatively, "I know you. I do know you. But—who—what are you?"

"You know me as well as yourself. But you must find out what I am. That is for you. I cannot tell you."

Prue bent her head and, looking now at her own hands in her lap, said, "Why can't Richard ever hear you? Why can't he see you now?" Beside her, Richard stiffened.

"It is for Richard to find me." The leaves suddenly rustled in a stronger gust of wind. The voice from the saplings grew louder. "I have brought you here to learn to know me. And you must learn for yourselves. Peter must learn to remember me later on. You must learn to see me clear. Already you have begun to see me, Prue. But Richard cannot yet even hear when I speak to him."

"And if he should not learn?" Prue's voice was almost a whisper.

"Then he will be lost. He will come home in the end, but he will come by a different route. He will come

112

home, but he will not be Richard any more. Richard will be lost." The figure was no longer discernible. Above them the leaves rustled as the voice finished speaking. But it repeated, "—will be lost."

Richard rose to his knees, clutched Prue's shoulders, and shook her. In the white face his eyes stared. "What is it?" he said. "What is it? What did it mean, 'Richard will be lost'?" His hands trembled, and it did not sound like Richard's voice.

When he let his arms drop, Prue rubbed her shoulders absently. "Did you hear what it said?" He nodded. For the moment he could not speak any more. "It is only if you can't learn to know him. You see, already you are beginning to hear. You *will* learn, Richard. You must. Because how can you be lost if we all stay together?"

"You heard it, Prue? All the time?"

"Yes."

"And you saw—something—in those trees?"

He sat thinking for a long time. At last he lifted his head. "I don't like it. I don't like it at all. You see, I shall have to believe you now when you tell me you can see —someone. But I can't understand it." From this time on he became quiet and withdrawn, and as Prue and Peter could both see, he settled into an abiding melancholy. It was as if he had begun to lose hope.

After this their protector was with them more often. Prue and Peter could tell he was there, although they could not always see him. Sometimes they caught no more than a glimpse—a shadow on the grass. Sometimes they only heard the quiet voice. Once or twice they found him walking beside them, quite plain, it seemed. But they could not always tell whether it was a man or a woman or whether he was old or young. They only knew that it was right for this person to be there, and always he seemed to belong to the place where they were.

Prue began to wonder if he had always been there beside them. Perhaps only now was she learning to see and hear him as he expected. Often when she became aware of his presence, she looked at Richard. Occasionally, but very occasionally, Richard heard his voice. When he did, he became profoundly disturbed.

"Why do you mind?" she asked him. "It's good that you can hear. He wants you to hear."

"Who?" Richard said sharply. "You can't tell me. You can't say. Can't you see I *must* have an explanation? I *must* understand. Sometimes I think I'll go mad if neither of you can tell me. Give me an explanation, Prue. Give me one!" It was a cry for help. But neither Prue nor Peter had one to give.

For Prue the times when he was present were always periods of security and joy. But Richard remained uneasy and defensive, so often unaware of any presence but their own that he came to think himself an outsider of some kind.

Because their direction was made clear to them, they traveled quickly now, passing through many different places and changing climates. For a time they wandered through flat, warm lands of seemingly endless sunshine and no storms or high winds to break the soundless calm. Here they were often thirsty and were glad of the many wide and shallow lakes they came upon. The country was mainly rolling downs and undulating grasslands. All about them insects rose up from the grass, stirred by their passing. And with delight they recognized many of them.

Once, approaching a stand of tall tree ferns, they were halted by the sound of a tremendous vibration. It drummed painfully in their ears, filling the air all about them with its din. When they approached cautiously with their hands over their ears, they found the ferns were covered with cicadas. They were the same shape as the ones the children knew, but they were about four times the size, and their drumming four times as loud.

"Not as nice as the locusts in our gum tree at home," said Peter. He had stumbled over a hole in the caked earth where one of them had emerged. The hole, too, was four times the size of the ones their locusts made. But they also saw and recognized with joy familiar beetles, stick insects, dragonflies, and cockroaches. Once they even saw a butterfly.

They also saw many live creatures away out on the plain. But their protector kept them far away, and after their last experience none of them was eager to approach more closely. Drawing near to the lakes was the time of danger, since most of the animals—and really, they were more like reptiles—inhabited the marshy ground on the verges of the lakes. And the lakes, too, had their dangers, for once they saw the water swirl and caught sight of the long snout and hillocky little eyes of a big crocodile. In fact, all the huge creatures could swim and seemed more at home in the water than on land. Often they saw from the safety of some distant hill that the surface of a lake was boiling with great bodies. They remembered how nearly their end had come before and, unless told to do so, never approached the lakes no matter how thirsty they were. Generally speaking, there was a great stillness everywhere. Few sounds, except the occasional large insects, disturbed the drowsy calm of the long, warm days. But sometimes they would hear again the queer whistling or a more ominous rumbling and guessed that the titans by the lake were locked in battle.

Once they came to a clear and inviting spring in the middle of an open plain. They approached it gladly and were surprised that the edges of it bore so few signs of other drinkers. But when they put their faces to the water, they knew why. The water was hot and tasted of ink.

On another occasion they were resting in the middle of the day beside a tall grass tree, leaning against its springy roots, when the air suddenly grew dark, the sun was shadowed, and a great swishing passed by overhead. They looked up and then cowered motionless as a great dark shape flapped its way across the sky above them. It was enormous—far bigger than any bird they had ever seen. It had wings and a long neck with a small head and beak, which it stretched out in front as it flew, as a swan does. It had long, scaly legs that trailed behind and a kind of tail. But it did not have any feathers, and they were amazed that it could fly at all. They watched in silence as it flapped its precarious way out across the plain with its black shadow chasing it over the grass. And they saw it land with a splash in the shallow water of a small lake they had recently passed. For a time they saw its dark shape heaving about in the shallows. Then it disappeared.

Except that Richard remained quiet, saying little and altogether relinquishing his role of leader, it was a happy time. Prue could feel that with every step they took they drew nearer to the end. As she kept reminding Richard, they had only to stick together. At this period they felt themselves at all times taken care of, and the land they passed through basked in sunshine and peace.

They made their way across the endless plain, and the long, tranquil miles fell behind them. At night they slept in some soft clump of grass, wrapped in the knowledge of safety. During the day they moved on, drinking from the many clear pools when they were thirsty, eating berries or fruit they chanced to find, but hunger never bothered them. Somehow they remained healthy and strong and ate not from necessity but from choice.

Then, after many days, they began to have a sense that this period was coming to an end. The plain must soon finish, and what lay in store for them after that they could not even guess. They began to feel a faint uneasiness. They walked faster, rested less during the day, and slept for fewer hours during the night. It was Prue who first noticed that the horizon ahead, which for so long had been a clear, pellucid blue, had now become slightly hazy. A long line of murky gray concealed the division, sharp until now, where sky and land met. The grayness could conceal a mountain range, a stormy sea coast— anything. Remembering the last mountain range they had encountered, where each peak had belched death, they kept looking apprehensively at what lay ahead.

In spite of their pleasant surroundings, the sunshine, the beauty of the flowers among the grass, and the happy bustling of small animals and insects, their spirits sank lower with each passing day. The cloud, or whatever it was, that obscured the horizon, was growing bigger all the time. One day about noon they came to a patch of boggy ground in which grew thickets of the same plants they had seen in the marsh. There they stood, clusters of straight, hollow, reed-like sticks, with circlets of leaves, slim and a delicately pale green. But these thickets stood as high as ten feet or more and threw a cool green shade beneath them. They approached the first gladly, for the sun was at its hottest, and with depressed spirits, they became tired more easily. They went in among the shining stems and threw themselves on the springy ground. All about them little flowers of all colors grew in the cool dampness. For a long time nobody spoke. Prue found her eyes closing. But before they closed, she saw that Richard lay facing her with his legs stretched out and his back against two of the bamboo stems that grew side by side. These waved in the light breeze, and Richard was being gently rocked as he lay. Peter was beside her on her right, flat on his back with his legs and arms flung wide, his face to the sky. She thought he had fallen asleep immediately, for his eyes were fast shut and he was breathing slowly and deeply. She allowed herself to slide into sleep too. Her thoughts left her immediate surroundings and became mere fancies, which in their turn merged into dreams. The dreams were uneasy, full of dark and distant happenings, vague portents and confused indications of coming danger. For a time they persisted. Then, quite suddenly, they went, and she fell into a deep oblivion.

Some time later she had more dreams, but these were full of light and happiness. Now it seemed that wherever she turned, all was well. Gradually she floated into consciousness. She felt content and relaxed, as one does after a deep sleep, but before she opened her eyes she knew that now there was a fourth person in the thicket. And she knew without seeing that this person was beside her on her left hand. She felt no fear, but her nerves began to tingle. She took a deep breath and opened her eyes. The glade still hummed with midday calm. Facing her, Richard slept and his palms lay upturned on the grass on either side of him. Lying so, he looked vulnerable and helpless. Peter still slept also in complete abandon, but there was no suggestion of helplessness in his spread-eagled attitude. It was the careless rest of complete confidence.

She allowed her eyes to slide to the left. Two long, slim legs lay stretched out and crossed at the ankles beside hers. They were covered as far down as the calf with a shimmering yellow material, which was untidily scattered with numbers of the little flowers she had noticed about the thicket. They had been picked halfway down the stem and lay about in confusion, but they showed no signs of wilting. The feet were white and fine but well-muscled. Prue turned her head and allowed her glance to travel up the yellow garment. The flowers were scattered everywhere, and a bunch of them was lightly clasped by the two hands that lay folded in the lap. Prue lifted her head. It was a woman who sat beside her, whether old or young she could not tell. The shoulders were covered with a scarf of silver lace that, in the deeper shadow, looked fine as cobweb. There were seed pearls along its strands, as cobwebs have on frosty mornings. It hung in gossamer folds in front of her and lay lightly about the heaped flowers in her lap. But it was the head and face, poised with lifted chin on a long, strong neck, that drew Prue's eyes like a magnet and would not let them go. Her hair was about shoulder length, slightly curling and of a kind of golden brown, and appeared at the moment entangled in the small green leaves of the bamboo above. Her face was pale, but the bones beneath the smooth skin were sharp and strong, the jawline sweeping generously from slightly pointed chin to just beneath the ear, where it joined the line of the cheek. Her eyes were large and gray and, like the other eyes Prue had recently seen, seemed to be lit by a strong light from deep within. They rested on her now, warm and enveloping. The wide mouth was slightly smiling. It was a face that revealed an infinite strength softened by an infinite patience.

In that first intense glimpse Prue thought wildly that it was her mother. Then, because she could not hold the constant gaze any longer, she looked away. When she looked back, it was no longer like her mother. It was a face that she had never seen before.

The woman spoke. "You know me," she said in a clear voice. And it was not a question.

Prue began to say that she did not—and then stopped. She did know her. She had always known her and recently more closely than ever before. For a time she held that compelling gaze. Then she said, "I know you. But I don't know your name."

"I have no name. I have many names. But I come to you when I am needed. I have come before. And now you need me again."

Then Prue knew. "It is you who have been with us all the time," she said. "I know it is you, although you look different."

The woman smiled, and her face broke into a thousand tiny wrinkles that glowed with light. "You are learning to know me," she said.

"I had better wake the others," said Prue, who had a

feeling that the woman might vanish at any moment. It seemed very necessary that they should have this experience, too.

But the woman said, "You need not wake Peter. He is with me all the time."

Prue looked closely into her face and, made bold by its benign warmth, said, "And Richard? He has nearly learned to see you. Perhaps, today—?" She leaned forward. "You look so beautiful today."

"Wake him, then."

"Richard," said Prue, turning toward him. "Richard, wake up." She heard his even breathing check for a moment, then saw his chest expand in a long, indrawn breath. His eyelids fluttered, closed again, and opened slowly. They fixed on her for a moment, then moved around the glade, and came to rest on her again.

"M'm?" he said sleepily.

"Richard, look." She turned to the woman again. "Please say something to him."

"Richard, look at me. Try to see me." The quiet voice seemed to fill the glade.

The last vestiges of sleep fell away from Richard, and he sat bolt upright. He looked straight at the woman, then at every inch of the glade. "Who's that?" he shouted. "Where are you?"

The woman raised one hand, palm upward, and let it fall again. "You see?" she said to Prue. "He cannot. He must try harder."

"He must," said Prue in anguish. "Richard, look!"

Again he looked about him, and his head moved in little jerks, like an animal scenting danger.

"He has not learned yet, and your time is running out.

121

I tell you he must try harder."

"He will. He will," said Prue. "He can hear you, can't he?"

Richard was on his feet. "I can see everything there is to see. I can see everything a rational person can be expected to see in this place. I hope I never see anything else." He was shouting and he woke Peter.

Seeing he was awake, Prue said, "Tell him, Peter."

Peter looked at the woman without surprise, as if he expected her to be there. Then he looked up at Richard. "She's there, Richard. And she's just like Mum. You just can't see her." His voice was quite matter of fact, and it did more to convince Richard than anything Prue could have said.

Slowly Richard sank back on to the ground. When he spoke, gazing all about him, his voice was truculent. "Then tell me where we are, where we're going, and when we're going to get home. Are we going to get home?"

"You are where you have always been, as I hoped you would have understood by now," said the woman. "You will at least understand this: you are making your way back and you are going toward where you came from."

Richard suddenly shouted, "I said—are we going to get home?"

It was a long time before the woman spoke. "You are already home," she said. "You have never left it. All you have to do is to recognize it. *Look at me.*" The last words came like a crack of thunder.

Richard jumped, torn between fear and fury. His eyes, guided by the ringing words, were right on her. His mouth trembled, and he was going to speak. But he shut his eyes and put his hands over his face.

"Ah!" It was a cry of disgust. He threw himself on the ground, clutching at the tussocks of grass.

"You did ask," said Peter mildly. Then he got up, went over to the woman, and sat down beside her. She lifted one hand from her lap and placed it on his head. They might have sat just so a hundred times before. Peter said, "How much longer?"

"Not long." Her voice had softened to a kind of croon. "But the next part will be hard and, after that, dangerous. What happens then will depend." She stopped and seemed to be looking into the distance.

"On what?" Peter slid his head from under her hand and looked into her face.

"On you and Prue and Richard. Most of all, on Richard. *I* do not know."

"Will you—be there?" said Prue with a slight gulp.

"I am always there. You know this. Peter knows this. Whatever happens I shall be there, and it will be all right in the end. But I cannot order events."

"You will take care of us?" asked Prue.

The woman now turned her head toward Prue, leaning slightly forward. "Yes," she said.

Perhaps she had gazed too long into the woman's extraordinary eyes, for Prue felt a film come over her own. She blinked several times and rubbed them. When she looked again, the bamboo stems were waving and a cloud of golden pollen hung in the air, but she could no longer see the woman.

"Come on," said Peter from the edge of the thicket. "Hurry."

She got up and walked over to Richard, who lay on his

stomach on the ground. She bent over him. "Richard," she said. "Richard, it's time to go."

Slowly he rolled over, sat up, and stared into her face. His look was so blank, so helpless, that she put out her hands to him. He took them and she pulled him up. When he was standing beside her, still with that dazed look, she said, "Come on, Richard, we'll go together." They walked out of the thicket hand in hand, and it was Prue who led and Richard who followed.

[13]

THEY WENT ON, and for a time they neither heard the voice nor saw anything of their protector. The gray haze in the distance grew larger and appeared more ominous all the time, but long before they reached it and whatever it was that the haze concealed, they left the plain.

The grassy downs began to diminish, the clumps of trees became fewer, and all the animal and insect life of the plain fell behind them. The silence, which before had been one of the forms of peace, now grew oppressive. It rang in the ear like a silent bell. It seemed heavy with a message it could not deliver. And the nights became shorter and the days grew warmer. The earth by degrees turned to sand and the vegetation ceased altogether. The mild undulations of the preceding countryside, which they had enjoyed, turned to sand dunes, and tramping up one after another was hard work. They grew thirsty as the heat increased, and now the lakes became fewer. The streams stopped running, and it became a case of going from one source of available water to another.

124

Their skins became dark with the sun, their hair bleached, and their lips dry and encrusted. None of them asked why there were trudging over this inhospitable desert. None of them suggested returning to a pleasanter countryside. They all knew that their journey's end lay ahead and not behind. Once they came upon something dark moving in the sand ahead of them, and they approached with great caution, because there was no knowing what this hostile country might produce. It turned out to be a lizard, basking on a half-exposed rock. It looked like a goanna, but it was bigger than any goanna they had ever imagined. As they watched, motionless behind the intervening dune, they saw it lift its head. A forked tongue flicked in and out once or twice, and they saw its eyes searching busily.

"Keep still," said Peter. "It's smelling us."

But after a time it dropped its head and appeared to go to sleep. Now they did not know whether to try to go past or stay where they were. In the end it was the lizard that made the decision. It got up, switched its long tail once and waddled off, and they watched it until it disappeared, a dark speck in the dazzling expanse of sand. Then they moved forward and found that it had been resting by a small water hole under the rock. The water tasted a little odd, and a thin film of grease was floating on its surface, but they were very thirsty, and they drank it. The slight twinges they all suffered afterward were a small price for having been able to quench their thirst. After that they watched carefully for the great goannas, knowing that where they were would be water. But they saw only two more and these were smaller, and so were the water holes they haunted.

The desert seemed never-ending to them. By day, under the searing sun, thinking of nothing but the next time they would be able to drink, they walked in a dream that was more of a nightmare. Prue and Peter shuffled along somehow, but Richard stumbled often, and they had to stop frequently and help him up. They did not speak because their mouths were too dry and speaking was painful. But they kept on because, even if Richard did, Prue and Peter never doubted that this was what they should do.

The gray horizon loomed higher and covered more of the sky ahead. They still regarded it with dread, but now there was no joy in lingering where they were. Each day reduced their speed. Each day produced more waking fancies in their minds, and they began to welcome these, for painful though many of them were, they offered an escape from their immediate surroundings. The nights were what they lived for, and when the sun went down and the daylight drained from the barren dunes, they lay down where they were in the warm sand and felt it grow cool beneath them before they drifted into a heavy and dreamless sleep.

At last the dunes began to give way to rocky outcrops. Here and there piles of tumbled rock, angular and glittering, crowned a dune, and when they saw them they made for them because they cast a shadow. Their progress was very slow indeed. After seemingly endless walking and getting no closer, they reached one of the rocky piles and sank down in the shadow, leaning gratefully against the black rock. Even Peter, whose small body was lightly borne on his wiry legs, had taken his last step. Richard's eyes were closed. It would be a long time before he could move again.

Prue had been walking—if her stumbling shuffle could be called walking—immersed in one of the crowding fancies of the last few days. In her mind she had been struggling to save her mother's house from burning down. The whole of it was enveloped in white heat, but she knew she must get the papers from the front drawer of the desk, and her mother was standing beside her, saying, "Father told me to take them with me. He told me I shouldn't leave them in the desk. His will is there, too." And Prue, in her dream, kept saying, "I'll get it for you, Mum. Don't worry. It will be all right." And she kept making sallies toward the door of her father's office, only to be driven back time after time. She knew she must not be driven back, and at last she went through the fire, and she had her hand on the knob of the drawer when a great crippling pain swept through her and she felt all her muscles grow limp. She opened her eyes.

She was still sitting in the sand, but in the blessed shade of the rocks. There was a mark in the sand that her body had made—a scooped depression that led out of the shade into the sun. Out? No. The depression came out of the sun and into the shade. Someone had just pulled her into the shade. Richard and Peter were half-sitting, half-lying beside her. At first she thought they were dead, they were so still. But then she saw that they were breathing, but the breaths were so long and slow that their chests scarcely rose and fell at all. There was something that she was immensely pleased about, and at first she could not focus her mind to find out what it was. Then she knew. She was no longer thirsty. Heat and thirst had both left her, and she lay in a complete and blissful lassitude with no wish ever to move again. The granite rocks rose up all about her, and the one which threw the deepest, most encompassing shade was directly in front of her, and it was a lighter gray than the others. She knew that it was this rock, with its far-flung shadow, that had drawn them to this place. She looked at it through half-closed eyes and had the fancy that the irregularities in the higher part of the rock had the look of a human face. The rock, indeed, might have been a human shape, hung about with a heavy gray cape and hood. The face got mixed up with her recent dream and looked like the face of her mother.

"It's all right. I've got the papers," she heard herself say, and then woke up completely.

She was not surprised to find that it was not a rock at all that was shading them. It was their protector. He certainly leaned against one of the piles of rock, but he was enveloped in a cape that threw a gray shadow even on his face, so that his features had the hard angularity of granite. Now he was a man, and, as always, neither young nor old, yet in some elusive way both young and old.

"I knew you'd be here," she said without thinking.

"You needed me," he said, and his voice was a deep rumble.

She looked at him for a long time in silence. Then she said, "Who are you?"

He smiled, and she felt again the strange spasm her mind and body always felt when those eyes looked at her closely. "Surely you know?" he said.

She felt herself smiling in return into that familiar, granite-like face. She was no longer afraid to meet his eyes. "I seem to. But no words will come."

"You have known me all your life. But if I had not forced you to make this journey you might never have seen me as you see me now."

Not for a moment did she doubt that what he said was true, but she said, "Why?" and waited a long time for an answer.

Then he said, "There is a tide that flows, and we with it. That is why."

Momentarily it irritated her that he spoke in riddles, and she said, "I don't understand what you mean."

"You asked me and I told you. I did not expect you to understand. As you are now, you will never understand. You had better not try." He moved one of his work-worn hands, bent his hooded head, and began studying the palm. He seemed to have forgotten her.

She felt that she so nearly had the answer, but it was as she had said. No words would come. She did not think he meant to confuse her, but he was right. It was not possible to make her understand completely—as she could not make Richard understand. She sighed, feeling that some kind of revelation had been snatched from her. She remembered Richard and Peter and turned to see if they still slept.

Peter was sitting up, alert and bright-eyed, looking first at her and then at him. Richard's eyes were open, too, and he looked at her because she was all he could see, but perhaps he had heard, too, for his face bore the strained and anxious look she was beginning to recognize.

To her surprise Peter said, "You must know by now, Prue, but it's no good trying to say it in words. You never can."

Richard swung around on him with a kind of ferocity. "If you ask me, I'd say you've both gone mad."

Prue moved close to him. "Perhaps we have. But it's a funny kind of madness that makes sense somewhere, if only we could find out where. I think there'll be an ending, don't you, Peter?"

"If you mean," said Peter, "shall we find our way home, yes, we will, I think. And I'm not mad, Prue. You may be—after the bump on your head. That's what Richard thinks."

"Well, I'm not. And you know I'm not, because you can see him the same as I can." For a moment they were ordinary children again, arguing as they had once argued at home. As he always did now, Richard remained silent, but he watched them with more alertness than he had for some time. Perhaps their return to normal behavior gave him encouragement. Then Peter got up and walked away and left them. He went up to their protector and stood before him.

Richard said, "What's he up to now? What can he see over there?"

The gray, cloaked figure was still staring into his palm, as if what he saw there fascinated him. Peter bent over and peered into it too. After a time their protector raised his head. Prue was watching him, and he said to her. "It is very interesting, but it bothers me."

"What is it?" said Prue.

"Come and look."

She got up and was about to go to him when she remembered Richard. She held out her hand. "Come along, Richard. Come and look, too."

"You know I can never see anything." Richard spoke angrily, ignoring her outstretched hand.

"Perhaps this time you will. Come along." She took his

130

hand and pulled. At first he resisted, but as she continued to pull, he got up and went with her. Peter still stood with his head bent over the broad palm.

"Come," said their protector. "Look." She bent over, but Richard hung back.

"Let him look, too. This time he will see something, because it is what he is accustomed to see. But he must see everything. He must see me—if he can."

Prue lifted her head to the face above her. It was bent toward them, searching for something that perhaps it could not find. "Why?" she said. "Why is it so important?"

"Because he must know I am *there*."

"We can tell him. We know you are there."

"You have told him. Do you think he believes you? He does not trust you any more. He is slipping away from you, too."

There was a long pause. Prue looked at Richard. His face was as stony as the face that bent over them. But his eyes, unlike those others, were blank. He still held Prue's hand, and she felt his own, deathly cold. Then Prue said, "Why have I learned to see you and he hasn't? He's much cleverer than me."

"There are many reasons. I will give you a simple one. There is a garden around the house where you live. There is open ground nearby. Richard's feet never touch the ground. Think where he lives."

A sharp sound broke across the last words. It made Peter look around quickly. It made Prue catch her breath in sudden fear. But it was only Richard, laughing. "I told you it was mad," he said.

Their protector continued, as if he had not heard.

131

"Richard is one of many millions. If he learns to see me as you have, I shall know."

"What will you know?" said Prue, and something had happened to her voice.

"I shall know that those millions will continue, somehow, to flow on the tide I told you about."

"If not?" Prue's voice was the smallest whisper now.

"If not, they will cease to flow. They will have to come to me again as they once were. Even the millions cannot hinder the tide. They will move on, part of me, but no longer as themselves. I shall have to deal with them."

"And Richard?"

"Richard will tell me which it is to be. Come. Look."

Richard glanced around wildly and stiffened, as a horse will stiffen, pulling back on a halter. Prue gave his hand a tug. "Try, Richard," she said. "Just look where we're looking."

Slowly he relaxed and went forward. He bent down, looked at each of them in turn and leaned his head toward theirs.

[14]

THE HAND THEY PEERED INTO was of a curiously dry and parchment-like texture, and in the middle of it a darker patch seemed to be moving slightly, as if it had a life of its own. They looked more closely and saw that the dark patch was made up of tiny black particles, all moving frenziedly about one another. It was this tiny movement by myriads of black pinpoints that gave the impression of one general movement.

132

Above their heads the voice said, "It is a wonderful thing, what you are seeing. At first I cherished it because of its beauty and the spirit of it, but now I find it is spreading so fast I must soon deal with it. In some way I must deal with it before it spreads everywhere."

"Is it going to kill you?" said Peter, without looking up.

"You know that nothing can kill me. But unless it can see, in time, it will destroy itself. It will not be lost entirely. Nothing that is mine is ever completely lost. It all comes back to me in the end. But changed—changed." The voice above their bent heads ceased, and a great silence filled the air.

Prue pulled Richard closer. She put her face close to his and whispered, "Try to see, Richard. Try to see him before you look into his hand. Please try."

Like a sleep-walker Richard lifted his head. But his eyes had the blankness of the sleep-walker still, and presently he lowered his head. "I can't see anything at all," he said.

"Look into his hand, then," said Prue, and she put her arm around his shoulder as he bent over, for she was full of pity for him.

Peter was already staring, transfixed, into the open palm, and presently in a new voice Richard said, "I think I can see something. I can see things moving about. Millions of things moving about."

"Look closely," said the voice above them. "Look closely, all three of you, and I will show you."

Then there was silence again, and they bent their heads until they were cupped in the upturned palm, which now seemed big enough to hold all three. Prue's head began to swim in the way it had before, and her headache returned. But, as she had been told to, she continued to look, and the little particles seemed to move faster than ever. They grew bigger, and she put out both her hands and held fast to Peter on one side and Richard on the other.

The palm seemed to be growing immense, spreading out on all sides of them until they could no longer see where it ended. The gray surface altered and changed from parchment to brown, from brown to pale yellow, and from pale yellow to a kind of patchwork of gray and green and black and brown. On the patchwork the particles had grown very big—almost their own size, and the movement of them was familiar. Everything about them was familiar. Prue blinked, gasped, and found herself standing in a roadway. It was as if she had woken at last from a long sleep. What had gone before was no more than a dream. She laughed aloud with relief and found that Richard and Peter stood beside her, also laughing. They, too, must have put the dream behind them, for they blinked and looked about, and at last Richard took a huge breath and said with a ring of happiness in his voice, "We're home. At last we're home." And they hugged one another and danced in the middle of the road.

The blare of a motor horn made them jump, and they ran to the side as the car went past.

"Funny," said Peter. "Didn't hear it come."

"Didn't hear it go, either, only the swish of air," said Richard. "And it was a new model. Wonder what it was." Then he took each of them by the arm. "Come on. Let's go home. I think we're quite near your house, though heaven knows how we got there." The old Richard was back, happy, confident, and in control once more.

Somewhere, deep inside her skull, Prue's head still ached. She looked at Peter and saw that he was looking about as he walked, alert like a bird. But he went happily enough where Richard indicated.

The road was familiar. She could not quite place it. For the moment she was still slightly confused, but she was sure that in a minute, just round the next corner, she would know exactly where she was. It was a side road somewhere. Somewhere very near was a place she knew well. A few of the houses on either side of it were familiar, even if they were a lot shabbier than she seemed to remember. But in many places there were new houses. They were more or less similar to each other, but in all of them there was something strange about the design. Most of them were of a kind of concrete, with metal window frames and doorways, and this was not a particularly strange construction. It was the general design, the placing of them, that was unusual.

Richard said, "Funny kind of architecture they've got here. Like modern styles run mad."

Then Peter said, "I know where we are. Bet there's a park around the next corner."

They reached the corner, turned it, and, sure enough, the park was there. Prue, too, had thought she would recognize the park and would have said it was only a few blocks from their own house. But when they saw it they stopped, frowning and gazing at the great trees that lined the roadside.

"That's not right," said Peter. "Those ought to be little

135

tiny plants with tree guards. And flowers all around them. That's what they ought to be."

"If your home's near here, where is it?" said Richard quickly. He was in a fever of impatience, and Prue suddenly realized that now, as soon as he reached home, he would know about his mother. "Come on," he said again. "Quickly." And he started to run.

But Peter said, "Hi, this way. Through the park's quickest." He led them into the park, cutting diagonally across the corner. It was quite a large park, full of Morton Bay figs and tall gum trees. The grass beneath them was brown with the passage of many feet, and on benches in the shade many people were sitting. They were all old people, some of them very old, and they filled the benches. It was a warm summer's day and the shade was welcome. The old people sat there not moving, as if they had been sitting there a long time. Some of them wore trousers and jackets, but whether they were men or women or both, it was hard to discover. Others, and again they could have been either men or women, wore long, shapeless garments, some in quite bright colors, and they must have been wonderfully cool on this warm day and easy to put on and off.

Peter stood in the middle of a wide path under the overhanging branches of a fig tree, and said sharply, "It's not right. It isn't like this. I *know* where we are, and it's wrong." Around him, swinging from the branches, the long aerial roots of the fig hung down, searching for the ground.

Richard had recovered his spirits and his optimism, and he said, "You've made a mistake, that's all. Easily done, when you've been away so long. If we can't find

136

our way, we'll ask someone. Anyway, as soon as we find a public telephone, I'm going to ring up." It was the old Richard—in charge, resourceful, and confident.

Prue, who had been caught up in Peter's bewilderment, found herself infected with Richard's perfect assurance. "Come on then," she said. "We'll find one the other side of the park somewhere and tell Mum we're here." The words sounded so homely, so ordinary, and everyday, that they all felt suddenly sure that it was only a matter of time—a very short time—before they would be among their old familiar things. Peter pushed his doubts behind him, and they hurried on through the park. The old people sat about everywhere, and Richard went up to a group of them who were on a bench near the path. He approached the end one, who wore a long coat of some synthetic material. They saw now that all their garments were of synthetics of various kinds. The old man was staring idly into the sun-dappled branches above. He had a kind, but melancholy face and washed-out blue eyes. One side of his face between the cheek bone and the ear was marked by a deep red birthmark.

"Excuse me," said Richard.

All the old people on the bench turned their heads to look at him. Prue and Peter stood back, with a strange reluctance to approach too closely. The old man lifted his head, returning the smile. They noticed that his teeth appeared to be perfect. "What can I do for you, boy?" he said, and sounded surprised.

"I wondered if you had the time?"

The old man smiled. "All the time in the world."

"I mean—I've lost my watch. Could you tell me the time, please?"

All the old people were smiling, and now they all shook out their left wrists and looked at their watches. "Half-past four," said the old man, and all the old people nodded and resumed their former positions. "Nearly time for them to come for us." And they all nodded again. The prospect did not appear to give them any particular satisfaction. Indeed, their whole appearance was one of resigned apathy.

"Thank you very much," said Richard, and they walked on. Prue turned to look once more at the old man. She heard him say to the others, "Why ask us, eh? They know it all better than we do." But he seemed pleased.

It did not take them long to cross the park. They had somehow expected the street on the far side to be like the one they had left: asphalt and of no more than three cars' width; and they were surprised to find it a wide concrete highway with six traffic lanes. On either side the houses stood well back from the road, and grass and shrubberies separated them from the traffic. The strange thing was that the highway was empty. But a little way ahead there were traffic lights and a cross street, and from time to time cars crossed at right angles.

"Which way?" said Richard, as they emerged on to the sidewalk.

"This way," said Peter, turning left. Then he stopped and looked up and down the highway. "I think," he added, and then said to Prue, "what do you think?"

"It's different," said Prue. "I'm sure I know where we are, but it's different." She looked about as Peter had done and then said, "But I'm pretty sure we should go this way." And she turned left.

"Come along then," said Richard. "We'll hurry."

For some time they walked up the wide highway. And once a woman came out into a garden and watered a plant, and once a delivery van came up silently behind them, and a man got out and delivered a parcel to one of the houses. Then he drove off, and they did not hear the car start, nor the gears being changed, but only the sound of the tires hissing on the road, and they felt the breeze as it passed. Richard looked at it with interest. "New," he said. "I wonder what it runs on? I wonder if it's one of the nuclear-powered ones they're always talking about."

"Whatever it is," said Prue, "it's nicer than the smelly old petrol ones."

When they had been walking for perhaps twenty minutes and could see a cluster of shops and buildings not far ahead, they became aware of a faint hissing sound in the air. It grew louder as they listened. "What's that?" said Peter, and stopped to look back up the highway.

At first they could see nothing, but the hissing grew louder still, and then a few vehicles began appearing. They moved soundlessly, like the van. They came in both directions, and most of them rushed past at speed, but one or two turned in at the rows of houses. More and more came until the highway was thick with traffic, and they realized that the noise like a giant whispering had been simply the sound of a multitude of wheels revolving at speed on the hard surface of the road. There was no sound of engines at all, and where the road had been empty a few minutes before, it was now full of vehicles.

"Bumper to bumper," said Richard. "Fancy our thinking there was so little motor traffic about."

"Is it *motor* traffic?" said Peter. "Doesn't smell like it, and it doesn't sound like it."

"As a matter of fact," said Prue. "If they're motor cars, they look different, too."

There were still vehicles everywhere when they reached the shops. They left the highway, which turned off in a great sweep to the left, and walked along a narrow street. Here among the shops there were people thick on the sidewalks, pouring out of the shops, emerging in a stream from the business buildings, talking, bustling, lugging parcels. It was a familiar scene, and it was a familiar place. Prue suddenly said, "I think these are our shops, where Mum does the shopping. Don't you, Peter?"

He nodded. He had been gazing, absorbed, into the shop windows. "But I've never seen so many people before," he said, and returned again to the study of the shop windows.

Richard suddenly laughed. "Of course," he said. "It's peak hour traffic. Silly of us not to think of that."

"So it is," said Prue. "It would be about time." But she did not sound as convinced as Richard, and after a moment she said, "All the same, there are a lot of people. There are a *lot* of people. More than I've ever seen, even in rush hour."

"Perhaps they're all out today," said Richard casually. "Never mind, it doesn't matter. The important thing is to get home. Are you sure you know the way now, Prue, or shall I ring up? There's no point ringing if we're quite near."

"We're quite near," said Prue, and a sort of bubbling excitement began inside her at the thought of being so nearly home.

"Come on, then," said Richard. "Come on, Peter. What's so wonderful about shop windows?"

Peter came after them, but there was a rather dazed expression on his face. When he caught them up, he said, "I don't exactly know what's so wonderful. But something is." He tugged at Richard's shirt. "Something is, Richard," he said again.

But Richard was surging through the crowd, not worrying about anything but the way home. Prue panted along beside him and when they came to the next cross street said, "Turn right here, Richard."

They turned right, and after a little while left the shops and walked again among houses where people lived. Again, the familiar-looking houses were shabby and dilapidated, and the new ones looked strange and oddly shaped. Several times during their walk buses had passed them. They were huge, white buses, bigger and more streamlined than any they had ever seen, and they were all crammed with people. Now, when the rest of the traffic seemed to be growing less, another of these buses passed them silently. It left the shops and went over the crest of a hill. They followed and when they reached the crest saw the bus stationary at the roadside. A woman approached it from the nearest house at the same time that another woman dressed in a white uniform stepped out of the bus, carrying a small child in her arms. It must have been so small that it could not walk, for she handed it over to the other woman, who took it with what seemed like pleasure, bending over it and rocking it, before taking it into the house. The white uniformed woman returned to the bus, and it went on. As they walked, they saw it stop several times, and each time a

141

very small child was handed over to a waiting woman. They never caught up to the bus, so they could not be sure, but all the time it was in view, it appeared to be delivering very small children and babies.

"Just like a grocery van," said Peter.

"It looks to me like the bus from some kind of baby-minding place," said Richard. "I'd guess these are all mothers who work. Their babies are being returned after being minded all day. Do you know of an organization like that, Prue?"

She shook her head. "Only day nurseries like Peter and I went to when we were little. Nothing like this, where babies get delivered like parcels. Come on. Quick! Let's run." She was filled with a sudden great uneasiness and could not wait to get home.

They ran then, all of them together, for there was something catching in Prue's sudden wish for haste. She led them for block after block and around corners, first left, then right, and now she did not hesitate, for all the little streets were familiar, and she was nearly home. Around one more corner, up one more hill, and down the other side, and the red brick front wall of her house would be there behind the gum tree at the gate—right in front of her. Richard kept up, one step behind. Peter, although he ran too, was dropping back, for he looked about him as he ran.

Then, just as Prue turned the last corner and was starting to jog up the last hill between her and home, Peter shouted from behind, "Hold on. Wait."

They all stopped, their faces red and their chests going in and out. "What's the matter?" said Prue. She felt there must be no more delays, and it was odd that Peter was making one.

"I don't know," said Peter, and his eyes roved about, over the roadway, the footpaths, and the surrounding houses. "I don't know. But—but—there's something the matter. I don't like it."

Richard said, "Nonsense. How can it be wrong? If this is the way, let's go. Why are we waiting?" And he started off up to the crest of the hill. Prue and Peter followed him because they could think of no good reason to linger behind. When he reached the crest, he stopped, and he was still standing, not having moved at all when they caught up with him. They looked down where they knew the ground sloped away to a wide, flat plain. Their house had a long view over the whole plain, and at night the twinkling lights of the houses and the rows of street lights, like strings of pearls, were visible for miles. Their view was one of the best things about their house. They could never be built out, their father said.

The slope and the plain were still there in front of them, the long view was still there. But of the red brick wall of the house, and of the gum tree by the gate, of the gate itself, there was no sign. There was no sign that any house had ever been there. The whole plain was now a vast enclosure and appeared to be an airfield of some kind. Down on the flat part there were long buildings that could have been rows and rows of hangars. There were workshops and machinery sheds and garages and huge aluminum tanks that glittered in the sun. And the whole place swarmed with people and planes and helicopters and what looked like amphibians and hovercraft by the dozen. And they were all moving soundlessly about, coming in, going out, taxiing here and there. And little red vehicles like busy beetles followed them about. The people flowed in well directed streams everywhere.

143

It was like a vast and seething ants' nest. But there were no houses anywhere. No one lived there at all.

Prue pressed the back of her hand hard against her mouth. Then she began to whimper. She sank down until she was sitting on the sidewalk, her arms about her legs, her head buried in her knees. And she made little, stifled, snuffling sounds. Peter gave one strangled gulp and fell on his knees beside her, clasping her around the waist, pressing his face against her back. The whole of his small body shuddered.

Richard continued to stand, gazing at the plain. He ignored his cousins but said loudly, "You've made a mistake. That's what it is. You've made a mistake."

The other two did not hear him and would have taken no comfort if they had. They knew that they were lost indeed. For the first time since the accident they believed they would never find the way home. How can you find the way to something that is no longer there?

For a long time they remained like that. Richard, scanning the slope below with a puzzled frown, saw a group of people come out of the enclosure and make their way up the hill toward him. They must have been workmen, for they wore overalls with the Qantas Airline sign on them. They were talking, laughing, and, as he could hear, swearing from time to time. They sounded like any homing workmen he had ever heard, and their talk was of wages, football teams, and the winner of the four-thirty. So much he could hear as they drew nearer. All the sounds were reassuring, and he walked toward them as they came up the sidewalk.

"Do you mind telling me what that is down there?" he asked, as soon as they were near enough.

They looked at one another, their faces full of a mirthful wonder. "Well," said one. "Where've *you* been all your life?"

"That's the Western Airport, mate," said another. "What did you think it was?"

"Thanks," said Richard.

They walked on, and he heard one of them say, "Where d'you suppose he's sprung from? Must be one o' them little men from Mars," and they all laughed. He had forgotten Prue and Peter and swung around to call out to them to move, for they were right in the men's path. He himself was feeling better all the time. These were the sort of men he had always been familiar with. It seemed more and more certain that somewhere there had been a mistake. He opened his mouth to shout at Prue and Peter and then saw that it was too late. The men had already reached them. For a moment he thought they would be trodden on, for the men did not step aside. They went straight on, talking and laughing, over, on, or through Prue and Peter. And Prue and Peter were still in their sad little heap on the footpath, and the men had not seen them or, apparently, touched them. Richard felt a cold grip on his heart. Now he rushed toward them as panic-stricken as they.

They got up as he reached them, and together they ran out into the street. They looked once again at the vast plain with its seething mass of people below, turned, and ran blindly back the way they had come. They did not see the big white bus approaching. It had the Qantas sign on it, and it was making for the airfield. Perhaps the driver saw Richard, for an ear-splitting siren began to blow, and then the bus bore down on them, and the shriek was the shriek of air brakes violently applied. They all saw it suddenly, too late, and threw up their hands before their faces as it descended on them. There was a thundering, a sudden agony of terror, and a numb blackness.

[15]

Prue WAS LYING on her face on the sand, and it was night. On either side of her Richard and Peter lay motionless. The great granite rocks encircled them, but their protector was gone. Where he had been was nothing now but a white patch of moonlight.

She felt bruised and battered all over. She was conscious of having passed through some crisis, but what it was she could not remember. Neither could she remember how she came to be lying on the ground. She tried to think, but her head was aching again, and swirling clouds seemed to obscure her thoughts. She let herself sink back into semioblivion, her body limp, until she was conscious of nothing but her own weight pressing against the sand. Once again, filtering through her skin into the very middle of her body, she felt the sense of being protected. Her mind began to work again, and her memory came back. The picture of what she had just seen flooded into her mind. The people, the airfield, and worse than all the rest the sight of the place where her father's house should have been. She sat up, looked about, and saw with a great gush of relief that they were still in the desert, still among the granite rocks. It had been a dream she had no wish to repeat—for it was the very heart of desolation to find that there was no home to go back to.

Richard and Peter still slept soundly, and she waited quietly beside them until the dawn had broken and the first sunlight flowed across the desert sand and washed the gray rocks with light. Then, because she thought they must go on, she woke them. Peter woke completely and at once, gave a shiver and a kind of rueful little grin, and said he was glad it had been nothing but a dream. But Richard took a long time to wake, and when he did and looked about him and saw where they were, the light died out of his face, his body seemed to shrink, and he buried his face in his hands. It took Prue and Peter a long time to persuade him to get up and to begin walking again. If they had not kept constantly encouraging him and keeping his spirits up in whatever way they could, he would have sat there in the sand and perhaps would never have moved again. Even Peter could see the sickness of disappointment that he suffered from and pitied him.

"Did you see him? When you looked into his hand, did you see him?" Prue asked once, as they walked along.

"'I saw those horrible little insect things just before we got back—got—" His voice trailed off doubtfully. "That's all I saw," he added finally. "That's all there was to see."

She slid her arm through his. "Never mind. One day you will."

"Why shall I? Why must I see something that isn't there?"

Peter answered him. "Because he *is* there," he said.

"You keep saying it. But how can I believe it? We've

got to a place where nothing makes sense. Nothing's rational or logical. Nothing adds up. I think you and Prue have gone mad. And I can't stand it any more. I wish I were dead!" It was a shout of despair, and it silenced them.

After this, little by little, he retreated further and further into himself. He withdrew from them and lived only in some gray remoteness of his own. By degrees they were losing him as they had been told they would.

They left the rocks and padded out across the sand, making for the dark mass on the horizon. Gradually the sand gave place to solid earth, and there were low hills between which streams began to flow. Soon they were among high, tree-covered hills and walked on a rich, damp loam, springy with rotten vegetable matter. A scattering of trees towered overhead, solid trunks bearing spreading branches with leaves that soughed and drooped in the now almost constant rain. There was much undergrowth, and to Prue and Peter's joy they saw many birds and small animals. Once they caught sight of a very large brown animal among the distant trees and after that went with caution.

Toward the end of their second day, they reached the top of a long rise and found that the land on the other side sloped down, ending not far away at the bank of a big river that came gushing out of the foothills of a range of very high mountains. These were now just visible through the clouds, and sharp, snow-capped peaks emerged here and there. The river flowed strongly, but almost directly below them the land fell away into a deep gorge, into which the river tumbled, sliding like glass over a rocky brink and cascading in a tremendous waterfall to the shadowy depths below. All about a curtain of spray rose up, mingling with the rain and laying pearls on all the stunted trees and ferns that clung to the cliff sides. Its roaring filled their ears and hummed in their heads, making speech impossible.

Away to their left, far below between rocky cliffs, the river ran on, but they could not see where it went, for the night was beginning to come down.

Peter cupped his hands around his mouth and shouted, "We got to find somewhere to go. Come on." He began to go down the hill toward the steep edge of the gorge. Cautiously they followed him, going where he went, stepping where he stepped, and not looking at the gulch below or at the thickening shadows creeping up toward them.

After a time they found themselves on a narrow path that wound its way down the not quite sheer cliff. Damp fronds of herbage and clinging ferns wrapped about their legs as they went. On their left the glistening rocks rose up, higher and higher, and on their right the edge of the narrow path hung over an abyss. But it was a path of some kind, and something must have made it. And it was going downward. Peter went on at a steady, cautious pace, one hand on the rocky wall, his feet well in from the crumbling edge. They had been going down for a long time before the path began to widen. Then they straightened their backs and walked more freely. The rocky wall must at some time have suffered a tremendous upheaval, for there were great cracks in the rock face. The strata had slipped and big slabs of rock were jumbled untidily at all angles. In some of the cracks seeds had lodged, and trees were growing, clinging to the sloping rocks with big, muscular roots, their trunks at a forty-five degree angle overhanging the gorge. It was the upheaval that had caused the wider ledge they now stood on and had caused something else as well. In among the angled slabs of rock were apertures, black now in the fading light, but some of them quite large and with steep roofs like gothic churches. There were quite a number of them, and they offered safety and shelter for the night.

They went toward the largest opening, Peter, after a glance at Richard, going first. At the entrance he stopped and looked around.

"Careful," said Prue. "You don't know what might be inside." She and Richard closed up behind him, and immediately he disappeared from sight. Warm, strongly scented air was coming from the interior of the cave. Prue felt Richard's hand grasp her arm. There was no sound from inside at all.

Then, suddenly, there was swift movement all about their heads. The air flowing from the black cave mouth seemed to come alive. It swirled about them and, as Peter erupted from the darkness and cannoned into them, it became full of swiftly moving black objects. The smell became pungent and horrible. They ran together out of the mouth of the cave. Then they looked back. The opening was full of diving, swooping, soaring bats. It was evening and time for them to come out of the cave—and Peter had wakened them a little early. Prue clapped her hands over her ears as the bats swept past. They swooped out over the gorge into the floating spray, where they began flashing silently about in pursuit of their evening meal. For a time latecomers floated from the cave and away, one by one. Then—no more. Their high, thin shrieks, like threads of silver wire, came back from the great spaces of the gorge. The children turned toward each other and began to giggle. It was a high and nervous giggle, but it discharged the tension, and they looked at one another with kindness.

"Do we go in there?" said Richard at last. "After the bats?"

"The smell," said Prue.

Peter looked at them over his shoulder, and his teeth gleamed. "Don't suppose there'd be anything there but bats," he said. "An' they don't hurt."

He crept in again while they waited, and this time he came out quite soon. He spoke in his normal voice. "It's all right. A bit batty, and bat muck on the floor. But I think they've all gone, and it's quite a big cave, really, and there's sand where the bats don't seem to have made a muck. I felt it with my hand. It's quite warm in there, and it'd be nice for sleeping." He yawned, and suddenly they were all yawning. The cave, it seemed, offered safety and warmth and rest, and it was what they all wanted much more than they wanted a place that did not smell of bat.

"Come on, then," said Prue. "Let's go and sleep."

They bent down and went in, guided by Peter, and he led them far in among the rocks until the faint light at the entrance to the cave was no longer visible. Then he stopped and after a moment said, "Here's the sandy bit."

They were out of the rain and the air was warm and the very feel of the cave told them it was empty. They lay down on the sand, side by side, close enough to feel each other's presence, and a great peace crept over them.

"Nothing'll come," said Peter sleepily, "except the bats

in the morning. This is the bats' cave, but they won't mind us." Nobody asked how he knew. Some bits of knowledge he seemed to carry in his bones.

Before she went to sleep, Prue felt again the sense of comfort and safety—the sense of being looked after. And again the firm knowledge came to her that all was well. In the darkness she opened her eyes, expecting to see their protector. But there was nothing. She sighed and settled down. There was no need to look. She knew that he was all about them.

[16]

THE FIRST OF THE returning bats woke them. Soundless in flight, they made quite a commotion about settling down for the day. Squeaks and scufflings echoed around the cave. A shaft of light slanted in from the entrance and gave a slight illumination to the part where the children were. The cave stopped there, but the tilted slabs of rock that formed it had given it a high ceiling. There was still too much darkness for them to see how high it was. They were lying at the far end near the back wall, and the reason that this piece of sand was clear was that the rock arched, smooth and domed, above them, giving no foothold to bats.

They were grateful to the bats for allowing them the use of the cave, but they had no wish to share it with them, and they left their pad of warm sand and crept toward the light. The corner around which the light came was fairly low and narrow, but the cave opened out again into a kind of entrance hall, and here the daylight streamed in. The triangular entrance framed a magnificent prospect. Beyond the ledge, mist and spray steamed and frothed out of the gorge, whose far wall rose sheer and gleaming to a jagged finish, softened here and there along its rim by shrubs and wind-bent trees. Beyond this again the land rose up, gently at first, and then in layer on layer of green foothills to the towering mountain range itself, thrusting peak after peak out of the vegetation up to the airy realms of snow and ice, piercing the far horizon of the sky. Few clouds had gathered so early in the morning, and the sun shone from behind the peaks, bathing the children's side of the gorge in warmth and light. The foothills were still in shadow, but a steamy mist was rising from the distant treetops. Within the gorge the spray was spangled with diamonds, and a rainbow hung in the roaring void. They stepped out onto the ledge.

Richard hardly looked at the grandeur before him. He was pointing to the far peaks. "Look!" he said. "Look at that. We're back where we started," and a look of appalled horror came over his face.

They had seen the snowy peaks at their first glance, but they had not noticed what they saw now—that smoke was coming out of one of them.

"It's a volcano," said Peter. He said it in the same tone that Prue might have said, "Here's a cup of tea."

Richard suddenly came out of his gray solitude. "Of course it's a volcano. I'm not blind. But remember when we saw the last volcanoes? Remember that they nearly killed us? Perhaps it's the same one. I believe it is. I believe we aren't any nearer home than we were at first. We've been going around in circles, and now the volcanoes are going to finish us off. Somewhere here—

153

somewhere near us—" He looked round him wildly. "There's an enemy. Something—someone—that hates us. It's been playing with us. It's just waiting till it's good and ready, and it's going to finish us off. What about that voice of yours? That's our enemy. You see—it's just been waiting. Who or whatever owns that voice is going to do for us, and soon too." He was shouting wildly, and his eyes stared as if they saw already the enemy approaching. Prue put her arms around him. She could feel his muscles rigid and trembling. He was panting and the sweat came through the rags of his shirt.

"Poor Richard. Poor Richard," was all she said at first. Then, when she felt his muscles begin to relax, she said, "We have been going home. All the time we've been on our way home. I'm sure, Richard. And that volcano isn't the same. Remember around the others there was nothing growing? Look at all these forests. And the bats and the animals. Around the others there was none of that. Really, Richard, it is different."

His breathing grew slower, but he trembled still. He looked at her—at the top of the tangled brown head beside him. "Oh, Prue," he said at last. "Oh, Prue. I don't know." And he rested his chin on the top of her head. But even while he allowed her to comfort him, his eyes remained fixed on the volcano, as if it might take the opportunity to erupt if he let it out of his sight.

The echoes of his shouting had only just died away when, from behind them and very near, they heard a low growl. They had forgotten the other caves and they swung around, not knowing which way to go, if they had to run. In the entrance to a biggish cave next to their own, clear in the sunlight, a doglike animal was standing. It was about the size of an Alsatian, and it seemed to be made entirely of muscle and bone. It was standing completely revealed in the entrance, and they could see its long, whippy tail. It was higher in the rump than at the shoulder and its hind legs seemed very long, with an unexpected and pronounced joint not far from the foot. Its dog's head was very wide across the forehead, with small pointed ears, small yellow eyes, and a long, strong jaw. Its color was a kind of gray-brown, hard to see against the shadows of the cave, and it had stripes of black across its back. It was looking at them fixedly, its lips drawn back in a snarl and its huge mouth of white teeth bared. Along its back the hackles were up.

With no weapon of any kind they were no match for an animal like this. If they ran, it would catch them in two strides. If they stayed, it could pick them off when it was ready. It growled again and they all jumped.

"Keep still," said Peter quietly. "Don't move. It's got milk and it must have babies. It might go back to them. But don't move."

It seemed a lifetime that they stood there, rigid and scarcely breathing. The animal's eyes never wavered, and it stood as motionless as they did. Then, after an infinity of time the hackles along its back began to go down. The lip muscles relaxed and the lips came slowly down to cover those businesslike teeth. It made no move, and it never shifted its eyes, but eventually the look of ferocity died away. Richard moved his foot.

"Don't move," said Peter. "Still don't move. It's got to move first."

The whispered words had carried to the animal, and immediately it gave a growl and the lips were drawn back. But they had learned their lesson, and they did not move again, and presently the animal forgot to snarl. At last its eyes moved as it snapped at a fly. And perhaps it heard a noise from inside the cave, for its ears pricked and it turned slightly to look into the darkness behind it. Then it gave them one last, steady look, saw nothing to make it suspicious, turned and went into the cave, and they saw the high, striped rump and its stiff, curved tail. It was gone.

"What was it?" said Prue, after they had begun to breathe normally.

None of them knew. They had all seen pictures of something like it, but none of them could guess what anything that size could be. Richard said he thought it looked like one of those Tasmanian tigers. But he thought they were extinct, and he thought they were a much less formidable animal than this one seemed to be.

In spite of the animal, they stayed on the ledge all that day. Before very long the clouds began to roll up, blotting out the mountain range and the smoking volcano peak, descending to the forest, and encroaching on the small piece of blue sky directly above. Soon the sun had gone for good and it began to rain. After yesterday's wetting they did not enjoy the idea of setting forth along the narrow path with no foreseeable piece of shelter for the rest of the day. There were two other caves, apart from that belonging to the animal and the bat one, and the caves were warm and dry, so when the rain came down, they retreated to the rock wall and chose the largest of the remaining caves and crawled in. At this time of day the mouths of the caves were quite light, for the sun, when there was sun, shone right into them. This time they found nothing. The cave was quite shallow, so that they could see to its farthest corner, and although there were signs of some previous occupant—the remains of a grass nest and a collapsed tunnel in the sand—clearly there was nothing here now. The roof of the cave was high enough for them to sit comfortably, and when they sat, sheltered and dry, and looked above them, they understood why it was empty. A kind of chimney led upward, through which some light filtered. It was not possible to see the sky, but definitely it was an open top. The cave was not impregnable. As they sat there, a sudden burst of sound made them jump. Then they recognized it and laughed. A bird—probably a parrot—was sitting on top of the chimney and its morning song, loud rather than melodious, was being bounced down the chimney.

They spent most of that day in the empty cave, and the calls and songs of many birds came down their chimney. They did not mind how ugly the sounds were. They welcomed even the cockatoo-like shriekings, for they were familiar sounds, reminding them of home. They spent long periods sitting, looking out over the gorge, catching glimpses of the distant mountains in between the clouds of spray and once of the smoking peak. It appeared placid enough. And more than once they saw the big shapes of eagles, in and out of the spray, balanced on the air currents and eddies that rose from the depths below. It was partly because they had begun to feel in touch again with the things they knew that they found themselves unwilling to move on.

They returned to the bats' cave when the bats had left, because they knew they were safe there, and they were almost getting used to the smell.

THE NEXT MORNING they left the bats' cave again to find the rain streaming down. They moved straight over to the empty cave. The ledge was awash with puddles, and the overhanging tree was weighed down with its wet leaves, dripping into the chasm below. They knew that some time they would have to leave, or they would never get home. But not today. When they reached the entrance to the cave, they were surprised to find that there was light streaming, not into, but out of, the cave's entrance. Somewhere above there must be sunshine, and it must be coming down the chimney. Like moths to a light bulb, they crawled in.

The light was not coming down the chimney. That much they saw at once. It was being generated within the cave itself. The chimney was dark and the light blazed from the very middle of the cave. It gave out a gentle warmth. It may have been their own fancies that suggested there was a faint smell of flowers about the cave. At first the light dazzled them, and they could see nothing else. Then Prue and Peter saw that there was something in the center of the light. They were not particularly surprised when a voice spoke.

"My children, why are you still here?"

It was a quiet voice, and not unkind, but they knew that they must answer. Richard answered first. "I've seen the light, even if I haven't seen you." His voice was aggressive, with a kind of nervous truculence. He was backed against the opposite wall of the cave beside the opening. "And what does it matter to you if we're here or not?"

Prue put out a hand to stop him. They were both looking at him in dismay.

But the voice said, "I am always here, and you will see me next time, Richard." It was neither a promise nor a threat, but Prue felt her scalp crawling.

It was Peter who answered the question. "We're waiting till it stops raining."

"Then you will wait forever. It never stops raining here. Do you not want to go home?"

"Of course we do." It was Richard's voice, and it was angry.

But from out of the light the voice only said, "My poor Richard."

Prue said, "Yes. Oh, yes. It was because it seemed like home here that we stayed." She could see the figure more clearly now. At first she had mistaken it for a white bird, but now she saw that the feathers were a white cloak, flung around the tall figure of a woman. She was sitting on a slab of stone, leaning against the rock behind. Her arms, from which light glowed, spread out on either side, her hands rested lightly on the projecting rock. On her right side the cloak was flung back, revealing an underside of dazzling white down. Her head was bare, and light came from her hair as well.

Peter crossed the cave, settled himself in the soft folds of the cloak, and said, "How much longer?"

Prue saw her head bend toward him, saw her arm bring the cloak around to cover him, so that he was almost invisible in the foaming white down, and heard her say, "Soon. Quite soon now. But you must go."

Prue wanted to go up to her and be enfolded in that cloak as Peter was. But it would mean leaving Richard, who could not see her at all and who somehow thought of her as an enemy. She took Richard's hand, held it very tight, and stayed where she was. She fancied the cave suddenly became filled with the sound of bells, but it was their protector speaking again.

"You will go now. You will go down the path to the river, and you will follow the river along the open ground, through the forest until you come to the great lake. There you will see me. Richard, if you cannot see me now it will be the end. And then—I will take care of you." The voice boomed like a great bass bell on the last sentence. Then the sound of many bells filled the cave, chiming, tolling, tinkling, ringing; louder and louder, echoing around the walls, beating on the ear. And the light grew brighter and brighter until they were forced to shut their eyes. Gradually the sound of bells died away, the last echo faded, and they opened them again.

The cave was dark. Only a little light came through the opening, and from the chimney one or two white feathers floated down. Peter was the first to speak. "Oh, well," he said. "Come on." And he crawled to the opening.

But Richard said, "Why should we go? Why should we, if we don't want to—just because she told us to?"

" 'cos you won't be able to stay. That's why. Come on." Peter's backside disappeared from view.

Prue pulled him toward the entrance. "Come along, Richard. We can't leave you behind."

He stopped her, tightening his grip on her hand. "Would you? Prue, if I don't go, would you leave me?" He was peering into her face.

She could only nod. She knew, as Peter did, that it was not possible to stay. She let go Richard's hand and crawled after Peter. She did not see his face nor hear his quiet voice behind her say, "I see." Then he crawled after her.

All that day they clambered down the narrow path. And all that day it rained. The gorge began to widen, giving the riverbed more room. The noise of the falls grew less. It was a long day, but by the evening, with wobbling knees, they reached the bottom. On both sides of the river were wide, grassy banks, and scattered on these were many trees they knew—eucalypts, she-oaks, clumps of frilly green cassias, and wattles. The trees were filled with birds, chirruping, cooing, shrieking. Confidence returned. They camped that night beneath the cassias and for the first time dreamed of home.

Next day the river took them out of the rugged country into a land of rolling, heath-covered downs. It was a windy upland. In the distance the mountain range was still visible, the volcano still smoking, brooding, biding its time. But they no longer feared it. They had her promise, and they never doubted. They saw mobs of kangaroos feeding on the downs. They were bigger than any kangaroos they had ever seen. And they saw emus, and the emus were big, too, striding over the ground, useless wings raised and flopping. And several times they came upon little, mild-eyed wallabies that stood up on their hind legs to look, chewing busily, with black front paws hanging on their hairy chests.

"I like them best," said Peter. "I'd like one."

They slept that night in the open, and the almost perpetual rain turned into fog, blanketing sound, wrapping them in a private world where only the smells of herbs and growing things penetrated.

Next day the land began to slope downward, and the river narrowed again. The wild things were more plentiful and showed no fear nor any sign of animosity. They began to travel faster, for they all had the same sense of urgency. After a time they began to run, though they had no idea from what or where to.

About midday they saw the first signs of the forest, dark in the distance. The mountain range seemed to have followed them, and they could see it quite clearly again, sharp against the sky. The peaks had changed their position, and now the smoking peak soared above the others, dominating all. In the afternoon they reached the trees and found that they were eucalypts—their own bushland. It seemed suddenly important to be among them before dark, and they hurried on. Perhaps the animals of the downs had the same feeling, for many mobs of kangaroos and wallabies were coming down from the higher ground. Even the emus were moving nearer. About them now, on the fringe of the thick bush, were many small animals, all scampering and scuttling with a kind of aimless urgency. Once a more ponderous thumping came from a bush nearby, and out from it, at a dignified but brisk trot, came a hairy brown animal the size of a pig. It was low to the ground, waddling on short legs. Its little, almond-shaped eyes seemed of less use to it than its nose, which it kept close to the ground as it ran. They treated it with caution until Richard said he thought it was a wombat. All movement seemed to be directed to the middle of the forest.

The afternoon had grown very still. There was a heaviness in the air that weighed them down and made movement a labor. It lay on the spirits as well, and they did not speak at all as they hurried on. There were a number of insects in the air, and they, too, had come down and now flew and buzzed only a few inches above the ground. The thick rainclouds had dispersed, and by the time they left the open ground the sky was covered with an opaque, colorless gray that was neither cloud nor mist nor blue sky. The wind had completely dropped, and all the small sounds of animal and insect life became magnified, as if they had been made in some vast hall.

They slipped thankfully in among the trees and found that all around them was movement and bustle, as the animals from the open ground penetrated deeper and deeper into the shelter of the trees. Keeping as near to the river as they could, they did the same. When night came, they found shelter in the hollow trunk of a fallen tree. The rounded shape did not give them a very comfortable bed, but they felt that it protected them, though they did not know from what.

The riverbed had cleared a slice through the forest and now, in the darkness, the peak of the volcano was visible, illuminated by a rosy glow. The outline was clear against the radiant pink. It was a calm, steady light, which, if it had been from the west, might have lingered after the sunset.

"It's not spouting things," said Peter. "I'm going to sleep."

It was an uneasy sleep for them all, frequently disturbed by rustling sounds and the snapping of twigs, and sometimes by more alarming crashings. All the forest was awake. But they were as safe as they could make themselves, and they could do no more until daylight. They got what sleep they could, and from time to time

163

they would wake and find their muscles taut, their whole bodies ready for flight. Then they would reassure each other and sleep again.

[18]

Toward morning they were woken by the sound of crashing branches just beside their log. The opening, through which the first of the daylight filtered, showed them nothing. But the log began to move. It developed a rhythmic, rolling motion, rather as if it were afloat in a rough sea. Peter crawled to the entrance and looked cautiously out. Then he withdrew his head, screwed himself around in the log, and said, "Come and look. Don't make a noise."

The biggest animal they had ever seen was standing with its behind toward them at the far end of their log. It had obviously been rubbing against it. And now it stood gazing pensively into the river below. It was covered with coarse brown fur and had the hindquarters of a bear, except for a stumpy tail, but it was approximately the size of a rhinoceros. Its head was held a little lower than its rump, so that they could not see it in its present position. But now it began to move, and they watched it shamble away from the log, down to the river. They heard it drinking—long, slurping gulps—and they heard the water, like some subterranean river, gurgling into its interior. Then it turned, water dripping from its jowls, and they saw its head. Peter burst into a giggle and clapped his hand over his mouth.

164

It had the face of a rabbit, but magnified to the size of a beer barrel. The wobbling, divided top lip, the two sharp incisor teeth, the quivering nostrils were all rabbits' features. But as well, and apart from the tiny ears and wide, placid eyes, each cheek shot out sideways in an enormous pouch, as if it had a mouthful of all-day suckers. Enormous it might be, but no one could be afraid of an animal with a face like that. Nevertheless, they retreated into the log as it began to struggle up the bank. They felt it brush against the log, felt the log tremble, and watched it disappear into the forest again, its great backside rolling like a sailor's. Among so many animals they knew, they felt they should recognize this one. But nobody knew. It reminded them of many animals, but it was not quite like any of them.

"Anyway," said Peter, "fancy being frightened of that. You'd only have to be careful it didn't sit on you."

It was full daylight now, though the heavy atmosphere of yesterday was still upon them. If anything, it was more pronounced and the whole forest hung, silent and hushed, all the eucalyptus leaves pointing to the ground, immobile, and the strings of bark dangling from the trunks motionless, too. They left their log, walking carefully, making no noise. The forest glades were quiet now. Most of the animals had gone, and only one or two wallabies, a large goanna, and a family of the ratlike animals hurried along on the ground. A little distance ahead their large animal still crashed his way through the undergrowth. There was no sound of birds today, but in the branches overhead a number of possums, which should have been asleep, were swinging through the trees, and twice they saw koalas on the move, one with a baby on its back. The sense of urgency was everywhere, and they hurried too, breathless in the heavy air.

It was at the dead hour of the afternoon, when the day hangs between morning and night, that they first knew it had begun. Far away through the still forest they heard a distant rumbling. This was no animal, however big. It was not the roar of the waterfall in the gorge. It was something more distant, more muffled, but more fundamental and more terrifying. They stopped still and it grew louder. Louder and louder. Until it seemed all about them and they could not tell from which direction it came. They looked everywhere but saw nothing. Then, very slightly, they felt the ground shiver beneath them. At first, each of them thought it was himself, perhaps trembling with fear. But there came a rustling overhead, and they knew the trees had felt it too. For the first minute they stood paralyzed. Then the ground moved again, and around them the great trunks swayed. The rumbling became like an express train in a tunnel.

"Come on," screamed Peter, and ran for his life.

They ran, it seemed, for an eternity, and as they ran the ground heaved and thundered. Sometimes it seemed as if huge waves ran along the ground, and sometimes they ran uphill and sometimes down, and often they fell. Around them the trees bent and groaned, and here and there one split, with a scream of torn wood, and crashed down, bringing the branches of others with it. Several times they saw the forest floor split into gaping cracks and the trees teeter on the brink before they went over like bowing dancers into it, and sometimes the cracks closed up again and only a few branches were left, sticking ridiculously out of the ground. If one of these should

166

open beneath them they were lost, but they kept on because there was nothing else to do.

Peter stopped once. They had come to a piece of ground already shattered by the quakes, and a few twiggy branches protruding from the ground told them a tree had been engulfed. Beside it, numb with fright and cowering, was a gray baby wallaby. It would not move from the remains of the tree, and they guessed that its mother was down below, buried with the tree. Perhaps it had fallen out of her pouch. Perhaps she had thrown it out. But it was very small and helpless, and it was going to die. Peter scooped it up, stuffed it inside his shirt, and ran on.

By the time they came to the edge of the forest, the earthquakes had stopped. Their run had become a tottering stagger, and they breathed in a tortured wheeze. They scarcely noticed that it had stopped. But now their way was blocked. A great sheet of water spread out before them. A sea—an ocean—for it went to the horizon.

"The great lake!" said Prue, when she could speak again.

"And it's the end," said Peter. They moved nearer to one another and went slowly toward the shore.

When they reached the beach, they found that it was alive with animals. Kangaroos, wallabies, koalas, possums, lizards, wombats, rats, and many like the striped creature in the cave, and some like cats. Large, small, brown, black, fawn, red; they clustered on the brink of the lake, bouncing, scuttling, slinking—up and down the shore looking for a way of escape. And there, a mammoth among the others, even among the ten-foot kangaroos, was their friend from the log. He stood, perplexed and worried, a great brown mountain on the lake's edge, putting one paw after the other tentatively into the water.

But there were some that, with panic at their backs, did not let the water deter them, and even as the three children stood and watched, they plunged in, swimming out into the lake. Now they noticed that the water was full of bobbing heads and erect, desperate ears, and here and there a long, powerful brown back surging along, propelled by padded paws.

There was no thought of danger from the animals now, and the children ran out onto the sand, pushing the smaller animals aside as they went. Away from the trees they could see where the river flowed, brown and turgid, into the green waters of the lake. It was coming in huge waves, as if shaken out of the forest. Beyond it they saw again the mountain range, and it was aflame, and the sky above it was black with smoke and flashing red. The volcano was erupting, and they were thankful they had come so far from it.

"What shall we do?" shouted Prue. "Peter, what shall we do?"

His hand was supporting the wallaby in his shirt, and he turned his back on the volcano and said, "We've nothing to do. Only wait for her."

Richard made a strange, harsh sound, and they saw that he was laughing. "A big help," he said. "That's a big help. What we need is one small, fast helicopter."

As he spoke, the rumble came again, faint in the distance and growing louder as it drew nearer. Again the ground began to tremble. Around them the animals began making little short dashes in all directions. Some plunged into the water. But they did not get far. As the beach shook beneath them, the waters of the lake began to surge, as if the whole lake bed were being gently swung this way and that in increasing waves. The bobbing heads rose and fell with the water, and some, far out, began to disappear. Animals began blundering about them, and they clung together for support. The big brown beast was padding anxiously up and down the edge of the lake, and above the rumble they could hear it whimpering.

In the midst of the uproar Richard suddenly shouted, "What's that? Look! Look there. The river!"

Prue and Peter looked and saw that the river had taken on a kind of life of its own. Great walls of water were pouring into the lake and then being sucked back, to bank up out of sight among the trees, only to plunge down again meeting the waters of the lake in a great spout of foam and spray. Along the course of the river a dark haze was gathering, flowing downward along the surface of the water. Yet it was more substantial than a haze, more solid than a cloud. Shafts of light gleamed from it, and as they watched, it took on a vertical shape, the highest part alight with flames. It formed itself into a figure—a tall, black figure, striding over and through the surface of the water. The river surged around it, leaping up on either side as if it would grasp at the outspread arms. The eyes shone with a white light in the somber face, the hair, part vapor, part streaming black strands, flickered with red lights. It came toward the mouth of the river in flowing strides, and thunder clapped around it as it came.

"What is it?" shouted Richard again, and his face was gray.

"It's him," Peter shouted back. "He's coming. You see,

you can see him now."

Then Richard began screaming. And the screams formed themselves into words. "It's a hater! It's a hater! It's horrible. Get away! Come on. Get away!" And he turned and would have blundered off into the moving forest if Prue and Peter had not held him tight.

"No!" shouted Prue above the tumult. "No, Richard."

He looked at it once more, appalled, and they saw his lips move. Then he put his hands over his eyes and sank down between them. They stood over him and waited.

The lake's movement had been increasing all the time. The shallow water near their feet swirled from side to side. Now, as the turbulence of the river met it, as the black figure strode down to the waters of the lake, its motion became even more agitated. The whole surface rolled in gigantic curves of green this way and that. The motion began to change, the walls of water changed their course, and as they stood, helpless, among the panicked animals, the whole lake rose up and came toward them. For a moment the sky was blotted out by a translucent green wall. All the animals at the water's edge swung around and bolted for the forest. The brown mammoth gave one high shriek and, open-mouthed, gallumphed up the sand straight for them. They knew it did not see them, but they could not move. Deep in Prue's mind was the knowledge that she must not move. Then, out of the wall of water, striding toward them, bringing foam, cloud, and thunder with it, the figure came. It seemed surrounded by a great circle of light and glittering spray, and its arms, dripping water, streaming liquid fire, were held out to them. Prue was aware only of the eyes fixed on her, felt again the comfort and the knowledge that all was well, when they were enveloped, and the brown animal was swept, with tons of lake water, over the top of them all.

Prue felt herself picked up, rolled over and over, pressed deep into the ground, pounded, battered, tossed like a twig in the maelstrom until all sense of direction and self-preservation—all thought—was gone. She was nothing and could do nothing. She was an infinitesimal part of the elements that had engulfed her. She had lost her identity. She was no longer Prue. She no longer had a life of her own. She was a part—no more—of the basic design, of the very earth itself and of all the elements that were part of it. Her mind floated in suspense, spellbound, until the process of which she was part was complete. Until the great working-out was resolved. And little by little tranquility was restored. Little by little the sense of violent movement lessened, the thunderous noise diminished. Until all that was left was like the ringing in the ears after the final fortissimo chords of a symphony. The air about her—the space—vibrated still with the echo of what had passed. She became aware of her body again and felt the nerve-ends tingling from that gigantic chord.

After a long time she opened her eyes. She was lying in a familiar gray landscape. The dusty slope rose up into a pallid sky behind her. The gray and black monoliths stood in groups about her, and over all was the utter stillness, the emptiness, that she recognized. Nothing lived here but herself. But this time something was different. The oppression that she remembered feeling before had gone. The cold sensation of that earlier, complete desolation had vanished. Strangely, she felt now that she belonged here and it was right for her to be here. She looked about and saw that the slope behind was repeated far away by a similar slope in front of her, that she was lying near the foot of the long incline and that, in fact, it was more like a tremendous saucer. It did not occur to her to move or to take any action of any kind. Somewhere at the back of her mind was the knowledge that any development in the existing state of affairs would not be coming from her. All she had to do was to wait.

There was nowhere to look but at the featureless grayness and the black structures, which cast no shadow. But she slowly became aware that the appearance of the ground was changing. The dusty grayness began to look more solid, more substantial, and the gray was changing to a kind of parchment. She looked at the monoliths and saw that they had become smaller. As she watched, they became smaller still. As before, the whole landscape began to change round her. But this time instead of growing larger, it was shrinking. Or perhaps it was she who was growing bigger? Now she saw that the great saucer in which she lay began to look less like a saucer. But still its shape was familiar, though for a long time she did not know why. Then, when she had ceased to wonder, she suddenly knew. It was no saucer. It had become the palm of a great hand. And she knew whose hand it was, and she was filled with a great joy. This was what she must tell to Richard. This time she would not forget, because she knew now, for always, and the knowledge had become part of her.

She rolled over, knowing that he was somewhere near. And it seemed that she must have shut her eyes again, for after a time she opened them.

I T WAS NIGHT TIME. The night sounds of the bush were all about them. Subtly, insidiously, the smells of warm eucalyptus, sleeping flowers, and crushed herbs came to Prue's nostrils. She was warm, comfortable, and very sleepy. Slowly she surfaced from tremendous depths of sleep. The spark of her life was still all inward, absorbed with the depths she was leaving. Little by little they fell away. She became conscious of her body, of its well-being, and of the certainty of an outside world acting on her body. Her eyes began to see. The night was alive and calm about her. There were trees, whose shining trunks reached upward into the darkness. She could see the branches outlined against the stars and the silhouettes of long eucalyptus leaves hanging quiet. Nearby crickets chirped, somewhere there were frogs, and far away one mopoke called to another.

She was fully awake now, and she sat up. No night is ever totally dark, and overhead there were a million stars. She could see the forms of Peter and Richard lying on the ground beside her. Peter was curled up, comfortable, in a hollow, and the baby wallaby was curled in the crook of his arm. Richard lay spread out on his back, blank face to the sky and limbs spread untidily, as if he had fallen from a great height. He might have been dead, but she saw that he was breathing.

She got up cautiously, stepped out from between them and looked about. The bush spread out all about her, and the tall, smooth trunks rose up all round them. Yet in one direction there was a feeling of space and of untrammeled distance. Slowly she walked toward it.

She did not have to go very far before she saw that she was right. The bush stopped short, the ground fell away, and she looked out over a long plain far below. Here and there were twinkling lights, and far away on the horizon a great galaxy that blazed into the night sky. Many rows of little lights radiated from it over the plain. A thrill ran through her, her nostrils widened, and she filled her lungs. Then she turned and ran back through the trees.

"Richard! Peter!" she shouted. "Quick. Wake up. Come and see. The lights of Sydney. We can see the lights of Sydney."

Both boys jumped up. Peter shoved the wallaby inside his shirt. "Where?" said Richard. "Prue, where?" His voice trembled.

"Over there," she said, and pointed.

Without waiting to see if they followed, he ran off. They heard him give a great shout as he saw the lights, heard his feet pounding faster than ever. And then, as they followed him, heard a sudden, terrified scream. The footsteps ceased. And after an eternity of silence they heard a distant crash.

They were running as fast as they could, when Peter slithered to a stop and grabbed Prue. They had reached the edge of the plateau, and at their feet a great cliff fell to unseen depths. For a long time they stood, panting, gazing into the black emptiness below. No sound at all came up—not a crackle, not a whimper. Little by little the night sounds began again: the crickets, the frogs, and the night birds. Life flowed back into the temporary vacuum as the business of the night resumed. Far away the lights of Sydney twinkled.

Prue bent outward, cupped her hands, and shouted, "Richard!"

Again she shouted, "Richard!"

They waited, but no answer came. Then Peter turned and ran back into the bush. When Prue found him he was sitting, hands over ears and knees drawn up, at the foot of a great white eucalypt, whimpering and shivering. She felt herself drowning in a wave of pain. She opened her mouth and a thin, high sound came out of it. Over and over again the sound came and floated away in the bush, carrying the very heart and essence of all despair and sorrow.

When the first blackness of spirit had passed, they saw that the night was over and the new day had just begun. In the half light, quiet on a fallen log, she was sitting, watching them. Her cinnamon brown dress lay lightly in folds about her. Her hands lay, palm up, one in the other, in her lap. Her hair fell about her shoulders. When they saw her, the tranquil face broke into a smile.

Prue swallowed, brushed her eyes with the back of her hand, and took three strides to reach her side. "You did it!" she shouted. "You killed him! You said you would take care of him. You said everything would be all right. And you killed him. On purpose, you killed him. I hate you! I hate you! I hate you!" She burst into tears, dropped her face into her hands, and ran to the far side of the clearing. Peter watched her somberly. The wallaby was nuzzling his face, and at the sound of Prue's voice it climbed onto his shoulder, the small head pressed against his ear. When she was quiet, he got up and walked over to their protector. The wallaby leaped off his shoulder and into her lap. Here it curled up.

"We didn't expect it," he said. "Richard is—was—our friend. And our cousin. We didn't expect it. But—did you do it?"

She put one hand on the wallaby, and it gave a small crooning sound and curled closer.

"Peter, you know I did not," she said, and her voice was very quiet. "If you must have answers all the time, you cannot live—you do not want to live—where you cannot see cause and effect. Under such conditions Richard no longer wished to live. He told you so before."

"Is that why we thought we'd lost him earlier?" said Peter. "He sort of—went away?"

"He had lost touch with you because he had lost touch with me. I tried very hard to bring him back to me because I thought that if he could find his way back so could others. But he could not. He never learned to know me as Prue did. He could not see that he was part of me—of the earth he had forgotten to tread on. And where you do not understand, you fear and hate. And you see hate in everything about you. It is not possible to be as blind as this and still survive. You know that he was already lost to you. And he was lost to me, and so—lost."

"We didn't think you meant dead."

"Lost? Dead? What does it mean?" She looked closely into his face. "There is a tide, as I told you, and it is beyond my powers to stop it."

Prue had stopped sobbing. She said now, "But it's not fair. It isn't fair at all that we—Peter and me—should find our way back and Richard be lost. Richard was *better* than Peter and me."

"Prue, what makes you think I am here to deal out

justice? What has been, what is, and what will be are all that concern me. And in the end they are all the same."

Prue had raised her head and was watching her. She held out her hand.

"Come here, Prue."

Slowly Prue crossed the glade and stood beside Peter. Her face was tear-stained, and she stood rather stiffly and waited.

"I did not kill Richard. But it is true I knew this would happen. I could not have prevented it, and it was not right that I should."

"You said you would take care of him," Prue said again.

She leaned forward, the shining hair about her face. "I am taking care of him. He is mine now just as much as he ever was. And he is nearer to me now."

"He couldn't even see you," said Prue, and in defense of Richard her voice became indignant. "He looked and looked and he couldn't see you. How could he find you if he couldn't see you? And when he did—that last time when he did—" She gulped. "The only time he saw you was when you looked—you looked—" A shiver went through her. "You were terrible. He was afraid. He said you were a—a—"

"A hater," said Peter in a whisper. "He said you were a hater. But you aren't, are you?" He put out his hand and touched the cinnamon folds on her knee and withdrew it again very quickly. "You aren't a hater, are you?"

Her deep voice answered him. "I am not. He was totally wrong, yet so nearly right. He had my name, but the wrong way round. He had it, but he did not know because he had not been able to see for so long. As I was then was the only way he could see me. My children, I am not invisible. You learned to see me, Prue, as I hoped you would. And I am no hater, Peter. I neither hate nor love. But you are mine, and if you have learned this you will have learned all there is to know. It has been a long journey, Prue, finding your way home, but you have found it at last."

"Peter knew it," said Prue in a small voice. "Peter always knew it. He knew where to go."

"That was because he was small. All the small things know. But if they are like Richard they forget. Now that Peter is growing up, he will think he has forgotten, just as you had."

"I won't," said Peter.

"Yes, you will. But because of this journey you will only think you have forgotten. Beneath your thoughts and your memory you will know all the time. You will never forget, just as Prue will never forget."

"Who are you?" said Prue for the second time.

She bent forward. "You know who I am. And if you do not know there is no use my telling you. But you can trust me. I am the only thing you can always trust. As for Richard, he is still mine, and he is not lost any more." Then she smiled again, and the first long shaft of sunlight speared over the horizon and on to her face. They were dazzled. But she held out her arms, and they both took a step forward. They felt the arms close around them, and once again Prue knew that she was safe and that everything was all right. She held out her two hands and would have pressed closer. But there was nothing there. The log was empty. Peter stood beside her with the wallaby in his hands, and the sun, floating clear in the eastern sky, flooded the glade with light. Above their heads a kooka-burra began to laugh.

Prue twisted slowly on her heel, turning until she reached full circle. Her eyes, her ears, her nostrils, her very pores were open to the new day. She drew the morning air deep into her lungs. At last it was the bush she knew. She felt it in her bones.

[20]

A MAN IN A CAR found them on one of the dirt roads that led down to the plain. They were walking side by side as if they had already walked a very long way. He thought he had never seen such shabby clothes. A baby wallaby hopped beside the boy. He stopped the car beside them and said, "Where are you going?"

"Home," they said together. The boy gathered up the wallaby and stuffed it for safety inside his tattered shirt.

"And where's home?" he asked. They told him, rattling off the address as if it were one long word. As an afterthought Peter added the telephone number.

"You're a pretty long way from home, aren't you?" said the man. "How do you reckon getting there?"

"We've been walking," said Prue.

"So I see. Well, you can't walk all that way. Hop in and I'll take you to my place. We can ring up from there and see what your Mum and Dad have to say."

At half-past six that evening their mother and father called for them in the car. The man's wife wanted to give them tea, but they decided not to stay.

"I dunno," she said. "These kids. I did what I could for them, mind, but they wouldn't eat, hardly, and they didn't have anything to say for themselves. Just sat there, mostly. All day. And that young wallaby in the boy's shirt. Not very hygienic, I told him, but he didn't seem to want to take it out. Oh. No, thank you. Very kind of you, I'm sure. But we've been glad to help, haven't we, Dad? They looked so tired—sleepwalking, almost, Dad said. Not at all. Glad to have been of help."

Going home in the car their mother sat between them in the back. She held a wrist of each, as if she feared they might vanish again at any moment. Their father was obliged to sit by himself in the front and direct his conversation over his left shoulder.

"We had to sneak out of the house," he said, "after you rang on account of the reporters."

"Reporters?" they asked vaguely.

"Well, of course. You can't have two children vanishing off the face of the earth these days without being plagued by reporters."

"It was horrid," said their mother, with a little shiver. "They kept asking."

"That's just where we weren't," said Peter.

"What?" said their father.

"Off the face of the earth," said Peter. "We were on it all the time." He yawned and shut his eyes.

"Two children?" said Prue. She had been dreading the moment when it would be necessary to talk about Richard. It seemed to have come.

Their mother released their wrists and put her arms about their shoulders, drawing them closer. Their father

180

cleared his throat. Before Peter could wriggle himself free, he said, "You didn't know, then, what happened to Richard?"

"We saw—we knew—" It was hard for Prue to say what they knew. But their father, concerned with his own problem, seemed not to hear her.

"If you didn't know, I'm afraid we have bad news for you. Your mother and I hate to have to tell you now, but we may run into a reporter before we get into the house. Poor Richard died." If he had expected a reaction, he did not get it. Neither Prue nor Peter said anything. He went on. "He was near a swamp farther on from the scene of the accident. There'd been a fire, but we knew it was Richard because they found his cigarette lighter." As they still said nothing, he added, "You might as well know it all now, I suppose. Your Aunt Kate was found drowned in the car."

Prue said slowly, "Richard kept wondering about Aunt Kate. He would have minded terribly." After a time she said, "When did they find Richard?"

"Yesterday morning," said her father.

"Yesterday!" She leaned across her mother. "Peter, yesterday was when Richard—" She swallowed and then said, "We knew he died yesterday morning, but—"

Peter stopped stroking the wallaby, opened his eyes, and said, "How long have we been gone?"

"My poor child," said his mother, squeezing him tightly.

"Eight days exactly," said their father.

Peter's lips moved silently. Then he said, "It was seven days to the fire, Prue. And another to come down to the road."

"Yes, but—" Prue stopped, her eyes very wide.

"You see? All what we—all the way we went didn't take any time at all. Eight days is all it was, and seven of those were the days before. And today. And Richard died—when they say he died."

Their mother looked anxiously at each in turn and then said, "Hurry, please, Daddy."

After a time Prue said to Peter, "She took care of him after all, didn't she? He never had to know about Aunt Kate."

"She?" said her mother. "Who?"

But they could not tell her. It was all becoming very hazy, and Prue's head ached. She asked only one more question. As they drew near their house she said, "Mum, are we going home? To our house?"

"Of course, dear." Her mother gave her a startled look.

"Well, is there—would there be—an airport anywhere about?"

Then her mother put her hand on Prue's forehead and said that she must be feverish because everyone knew perfectly well that Mascot was the only airport and it was miles away.

Reporters seemed to spring up from the ground as they drove in at the front gate. Questions came like hail as they struggled out of the car. But their father swept them quickly in at the back door, and they heard him say briskly, "Yes, our two children have been found. They'd got lost after the accident and must have walked in a big circle. People do, when they get lost. Yes, quite well, apparently."

As soon as they got inside they called the doctor, who

said Prue had had slight concussion and that one never knew, but it seemed pretty right now. But they mustn't expect too much. Nobody quite knew what he meant by that, but it saved her many awkward questions.

When they told their parents not to be too sad for Richard because he had wanted to die, they were given warm milk and aspirin and told not to think about it now. They were asked one or two questions.

But it was hopeless to try and tell, and now they could scarcely remember. They had been on their way home, they said. Yes, all the time.

Two more things happened. Prue and Peter were walking through the park one day soon afterward on their way to the shops. The flower beds were newly planted and the little trees were growing splendidly in their guards. There were only little children in the park because school was not yet out. One little boy was scampering after a ball that his mother was throwing and shrieking with laughter as he fell on it. One of the throws brought him quite close to Prue and Peter. She grabbed Peter's arm as the child picked himself up. "Look, Peter," she said. "Look at his face."

They both looked at the deep red birthmark that stretched from the eye to the ear, all over one side of his face and knew that they had seen it before.

The child ran off, shrieking with delight, and they walked on.

One evening some months later a professor and his wife came to dinner. The professor had been a school friend of their father's. It was still light when they arrived, and the wallaby, who had thrived on suburban life, was bouncing about on the lawn, nibbling the rose bushes. The professor might not have noticed it if it had not bounded up to them and put its little black paws on his wife's skirt. So it was explained that it was Peter's pet that he had found on his way home after the terrible accident.

The professor bent down to pass the time of day with it, stopped, looked carefully, picked up the wallaby and turned it on its back, and said to his wife, "God bless my soul, Hilda, look at this. Now this is really interesting." He looked up at Peter's father. "This is most extraordinary. These little creatures were supposed to be extinct. I had no idea there were any still living. I'll have to get Peter to tell me exactly where he found it." They were both bending over the wallaby.

Peter's father laughed. "He won't tell you," he said. "Neither of them can tell us a thing. Prue, of course, is still a little confused. But all you'll find they'll say is that they were on their way home."

The wallaby, tired of reclining on its back, twisted itself away and bounded across the lawn to the flower bed where it started on another rose shoot.